Schrödinger's Wife

(and other possibilities)

T0100318

Schrödinger's Wife
(and other possibilities)

Pippa Goldschmidt

Goldsmiths
Press

Goldsmiths
UNIVERSITY OF LONDON

Contents

ALTERNATIVE GEOMETRIES

Let any number of women be represented as points in space and time, and you will always be able to find a surface that connects them. This was what Einstein's wife, whose name was Mileva Marić, was working on when she fell pregnant with their first child. (The one who disappeared from history. In other words, the girl.)

Nobody has ever bothered to test Mileva Marić's theory, until now.

Let the first woman be Valentina Tereshkova, and let her location in the space-time continuum be the occasion of her visit to the Royal Observatory in Edinburgh almost exactly a year after the Berlin Wall has come down. I'm a student at the Observatory, where I calculate how black holes and galaxies form in the early universe, and how to save enough money from my grant to buy some new jeans. On the day that Valentina Tereshkova is invited to the Observatory I'm chosen to show her around, even though I don't speak a word of Russian and she doesn't appear to understand English.

I only know one fact about Valentina Tereshkova but it's an important one; she was the first woman to travel into outer space. Back in 1963 when the Russians were still Soviets and when the Soviets were beating the Americans at the space race, she spent nearly three days orbiting the Earth in a Vostok rocket.

I've been instructed to show her the Observatory's two telescopes, one in each of the copper-domed towers at either end of the building. Nobody has actually looked through these telescopes for many years; in their way they're now as defunct as the Soviet Union and spend their days waiting for someone to come and dismantle them. We use up-to-date machinery for our research; new telescopes, cameras, satellites and so on, but these are all a long way from the Observatory itself. Right here it's somewhat more historic, and I imagine that Valentina Tereshkova might have encountered other, similar out-of-date chunks of metal; as I talk to her I picture old space rockets peacefully rusting into the black earth of the Caucasus.

Maybe it's because I know Valentina Tereshkova can't understand what I'm saying that I start to tell her about the bomb. How, in 1913, an unknown suffragette placed a bomb at the base of this tower, the subsequent explosion damaging the curved wall and injuring the woman herself, who left a trail of blood leading away from the Observatory and down the hill. I even tell Valentina Tereshkova about the handbag found at the scene, which contained some currant buns and a note fastened to it by a safety-pin saying 'Deeds not words', the suffragette slogan. I speculate about why the woman didn't eat the buns before the bomb went off; perhaps she was too nervous or perhaps they were an obscure political statement. Valentina Tereshkova nods at me, probably thinking that I'm explaining my PhD work on distant galaxies and black holes.

That is what I'm supposed to be telling her. I'm not supposed to be telling her about the suffragette bombing, as hidden a history as the black holes themselves, which can only be indirectly inferred from the way they disturb their surroundings, warping space-time into curved surfaces, as predicted by Einstein and subsequent physicists.

There is a persistent but undocumented rumour that Mileva Marić helped her husband with some of the trickier aspects of the maths in his work. I too have always been good at maths, and I can write a line of algebra that symbolises a surface extending to infinity in all directions. Valentina Tereshkova never went as far as infinity; in her Vostok rocket she reached an altitude of 200,000 metres, or about sixty times further from sea level than I've ever been.

In geometry you need more than one point to define a surface, so let the second point be occupied by the Austrian physicist Lise Meitner, sitting on her bed and scribbling notes in a hotel room somewhere in Stockholm. It is spring 1939. She was born in Vienna in the late nineteenth century to a Jewish family, and her original name was Elise, mutating at some unknown point in her childhood.

Lise Meitner spends most of her professional life at a science institute in Berlin, where initially she has to work in a basement, separated from the male scientists. (I say 'work' but she wasn't actually paid a salary for the first few years.)

Over time she's allowed to interact with the men, slowly and cautiously at first, in case they run from her like startled deer. She starts a lifelong collaboration with the chemist Otto Hahn, and in 1907 they set up a laboratory together.

At the beginning of the twentieth century an elegant experiment showed that almost all of an atom's mass is concentrated in a tiny nucleus at its centre. Sometimes this nucleus emits high energy radiation and particles, transforming itself in the process; the resulting daughter atom is now a different chemical element bearing no trace of its mother substance. It is this radioactive phenomenon that intrigues Lise Meitner.

In 1933 she has been living and working in Berlin for over twenty-five years and across Germany, Jewish scientists are dismissed from their jobs. Somehow she manages to hold onto hers; perhaps it's because she's Austrian and technically not subject to the laws of the Third Reich, or perhaps the relevant officials haven't noticed her because she's a woman. There's no way of finding out the right answer to the question without drawing attention to herself, and that would be very dangerous. But after Germany annexes Austria in 1938 and Austrian citizens automatically become German, she's altered from one identity to another and now all the laws of the Third Reich definitely apply to her.

The third woman in the continuum isn't a scientist. Not long after Lise Meitner leaves Vienna for Berlin, my grandmother is born in that city and she is known as Lisl, an adaptation of her birth name Elise.

In 1938 Lisl escapes from Vienna to London. At a time when hardly any Jewish adults are allowed to enter Britain from overseas, somehow (I don't know how) she obtains a visa which gives her permission to get a job as a domestic maid.

Let us imagine her at work, methodically removing the contents of a kitchen cupboard and setting the stacks of cups and saucers and plates and bowls on the floor, before wiping down the cupboard shelves first with a damp cloth and then a dry one. She has to rearrange the crockery in the cupboard several different times before she can close the door, because it will only fit if you do it the single right way and not one of the countless wrong ways. While she works, she is kneeling in front of this cupboard and trying not to think about what is happening in Austria. (But how can you not think when you do a task like this? How can your mind not fly off in all directions?) There's too much room inside her head and not enough in the cupboard.

In 1938 Lise Meitner escapes from Berlin to Stockholm, where she's been promised space to work in the physics laboratory at the Nobel Institute. Sweden is neutral territory, she should be safe here. But because the director of this laboratory doesn't approve of women physicists, she has no official status and, just as in Berlin thirty years before, she's confined to a basement. In a letter to Otto Hahn she writes, 'This place is unimaginably empty. There are no pumps, no capacitors, no ammeters, nothing to do experiments with.'

All she's managed to bring with her from Berlin are two small suitcases of summer clothes, and now it's winter and she's getting colder with every passing day. She writes to Otto Hahn again and asks him to post her woollens and her books. Meanwhile she sits in her basement.

But she'll manage. After all, she studies the atom. Too small to see even with the most powerful microscope, the atom still has enough space for these fascinating processes she's spent her life studying. If a nucleus were the size of a house fly, the surrounding atom would be as big as a cathedral. So why complain about being limited to this basement when she can think about what happens when atoms mutate?

The only home she has is a room in a rather down-at-heel hotel. Over the years she's stayed in many such places, become used to bedrooms with bathrooms a long chilly walk down a corridor, and meals provided at extra cost. Furnished bedrooms with two drawers for her underwear and a wardrobe, or maybe just a hook on the back of the door, for her dresses. A rickety table where she can spread out her books and papers, and a frayed rug on the floor to cover the holes in the linoleum. Small rooms – these rooms are never spacious – that require her to be quiet and orderly and neat. She has learned that this is how single women must live.

In 1939, Lise Meitner works on the problem of nuclear fission. Otto Hahn writes to her with baffling information about his latest experiment. When he bombards uranium atoms with neutrons, they seem to mutate into barium. She estimates that every time a single neutron hits a uranium atom, it is capable of breaking up into two smaller atoms of barium and krypton, and releasing more neutrons in a runaway chain reaction. In a bedroom so small she can touch the opposite walls while she is sitting down, and spending days silently by herself because nobody else will talk to her, Lise Meitner completes a calculation that will trigger the future atom bomb.

After the end of the war, when Otto Hahn is awarded the Nobel Prize for their collaborative work and she is over-looked, someone asks her if being Jewish has damaged her career. Lise Meitner answers, 'Being a woman is such a huge handicap that my religion has never mattered.' But she is wrong. Being Jewish in the Third Reich was the first stage of rendering her work invisible.

In the same month that I meet Valentina Tereshkova, my grandmother moves into an old people's home. When I visit her there, I find her sitting at a table and cutting up used greeting cards to make new ones. I watch as she manoeuvres the scissors, causing little pieces of coloured card to flutter down before she assembles them into a collage. My grandmother chats to me as she does this but she never tells me anything about her past, and about what – or whom – she left behind in Vienna. The collage is such a perfectly constructed flat surface it has no tell-tale gaps.

After I show Valentina Tereshkova around the Observatory, I go home and boil an egg for my supper. I crack open the egg and eat it, and cup the pieces of broken shell in the palm of my hand. A shell that once protected its contents from the rest of the universe; a miniature spacecraft.

The name of Mileva Marić's lost girl was Lieserl and she was born in 1902, somewhere in Serbia. It's not known when she died. As space-time expands and carries us all away from each other into our own separate futures, let us remember.

YELLOW

Margaret's first task is to decide what she means by the 'behaviour of fruit flies', and she realises their mating activities will have to be broken down into different stages and categorised before she can get to the tricky business of actually recording them. So she spends many days peering down her microscope and watching the flies go through their life cycles: hatch, crawl, eat, defecate, and mate.

Her PhD supervisor comes to check up on progress. 'Well?' he says, glancing around at the test tubes of yeast and flies, the bright light focused on the pedestal of the microscope, the jar of ether where the flies end up. Behind him stands the newest student in the team.

Margaret tells him she's made progress on identifying the mating process, which she now describes in terms of three stages: orientation, wing vibration and licking. She explains the initial orientation in which the male and female flies face each other, and if the female moves away, the male will follow her. She discusses the details of wing vibration, the male fly holding out first one wing and then the other at 90 degrees from his body before vibrating it. She describes the process of licking, the male fly extending his proboscis and licking the female's genitalia before actual copulation. Her supervisor nods, looks around again and leaves.

The newest student is still there. Now he clears his throat before speaking to her for the first time, suggesting they have tea in the common room. She accepts, and remembers to apologise for the pungent smell of yeast – the flies' favourite food – that clings to her even after she removes her lab coat.

Ten years ago, at one of the dances that took place on a regular basis. Margaret is wearing some borrowed shoes that pinch, and is trying to rub her heels surreptitiously without the other girls noticing. The rest of them are giggling, all apparently looking forward to the evening ahead, but she is very aware of the tightness of her smile.

When the men arrive, they bunch up on the far side of the hall. Without her glasses (left behind in her digs because they were deemed by the other girls to be off-putting) they all look worryingly alike, khaki being the dominant feature. She tries not to peer, she will have to get much closer to the men to be able to spot any identifying details.

'Oh Peggy, lighten up! You'll never catch a bloke looking like a wet weekend!'

But as the band strikes a new tune, a man approaches her. She positions her left hand on his shoulder in a reasonably accurate approximation of what the girls taught her, and as they shuffle around the dancefloor, she's able to move her feet safely out of the way of his. This close up, she can focus on purple smudges under his eyes and detect his smell:

a mingling of mothballs, sweat and beer. The hollow in the base of his throat is not unattractive.

'Care for a break?' he says to her when the music stops, and this hollow may be the reason she agrees. Sinking into the cool water of the night feels so welcome after the noisy fug of the dance hut and she's able to ease off the offending shoes. Then comes the inevitable offer to light her cigarette, which even she can guess is just an excuse for him to cup her hand in his. Leaning side by side against the wall of the hut means he can't see her, so she's talking to the night air as she tells him about her plans to return to Oxford when the war's over, and continue her zoology degree. When she says this, he makes an incredulous splutter, but she wants him to know what she finds so interesting about the natural world. Not the world of reports and chits and creased uniforms and water pipes at the end of the street. When she digs for victory, she tells him, she pauses after each spadeful to examine the exposed earthworms, she likes to watch them glide away from the light and back into their homes.

After she stops talking about the worms, she realises he has been silent for some time.

'Come on,' he tells her. She assumes they're going to dance again, but back in the hut she watches him stride towards another girl.

'Don't talk so flipping much. That's not what they're here for.' Barbara is keeping her company by the side of the dancefloor. They face the circling couples, some laughing, others looking almost grim with concentration. 'They don't want chapter and verse on your life, Peggy. You have to let the men lead if you want to get anywhere. Let them think they're in control.'

Now, Margaret talks about her flies to the newest student over more tea. He is quieter than most of the other students, perhaps because he is so much younger. This is the categorisation she can never avoid, one that divides them all into two mutually exclusive classes. Old enough to have experienced the war, or young enough for it to loom over their future, a station further down the track.

'How are you planning to record what you see?' He drinks his tea while gazing at her over the rim of the cup. She wonders if she looks at her flies in the same way, with openness and interest.

'I was a recording assistant at the BBC during the war, so I know how to operate a tape deck with split-second timing.' Then she explains how she's going to do it, with a tape and a metronome; the lengths of time spent by her flies on each of the three stages will be recorded as measurable intervals with the metronome ticking away in the background.

Eight years ago. The smell of the office, a possibly combustible mixture of dust, cigarettes and ambition. She is in here by herself practicing how to operate the tape deck, because she doesn't want to get it wrong. Click, the button is depressed. Another click, and it is released. Now she tries to synchronise it to the time pips being broadcast: click click click click click click –

The door opens. 'Miss Bastock! *Thought* you'd be hiding away in here,' the immensely self-satisfied tone of her boss fills the small room, 'I've got something for you.' She hopes it is related to work. But he pulls something out of his jacket pocket, a magician with a black-market rabbit, and she realises with a sinking heart that his movement has, just like her attempts with the tape deck, been rehearsed with a specific aim in mind. Something gauzy and filmy droops from his hands. 'Thought you might appreciate – ' he says, and stops, and holds out the fabric as if in supplication.

'Oh, I couldn't possibly, Mr Griffiths,' she pitches her voice higher than usual, and forces herself to smile demurely. She dares not risk annoying him because he's the section manager but how on earth can she accept a pair of stockings?

'Suppose any woman would be glad of – ' but he's faltering now. He comes further into the room and she has to lean against the tape deck to avoid him, the plastic buttons painful against the small of her back. He's looking not at her face but lower down. She remembers learning at university that there is a strong evolutionary advantage in the whites of eyes being so visible in *homo sapiens*. They indicate precisely where someone else is looking, so that you can follow their gaze and work out what they are hunting. This means you too can hunt it. Get to the prey before they do.

Successful hunting requires quick thinking, 'I'm sure another girl would appreciate them, how about Miss Dawson in news? She's always saying how much she'd love a pair of stockings!'

'Miss Dawson,' he repeats, 'Yes. Good suggestion.' His face flushes red in anticipation of further chase and possible conquest. She breathes out before silently apologising to Miss Dawson who, she hopes, will be equally as nimble on her feet.

Now, after so many weeks spent watching the flies, and before the actual recording of their mating activities gets properly underway, Margaret makes a much-needed and delayed trip to the hairdresser's which she generally dislikes because of the pretence involved. This time is no different and when she's led to the chair placed in front of the mirror, she gets an unpleasantly direct view of the hairdresser considering her hair.

'It's a bit mousy,' the hairdresser is picking up strands before letting them fall back onto her shoulders. She feels she ought to apologise for the bland colour of her hair, but she's never particularly cared one way or the other. 'How about going blonde?' the hairdresser points at a picture pinned to the wall; an improbably glamorous Hollywood starlet with a long fringe tumbling over one eye peers at her, 'It's quite straightforward! And very up to date.'

'I don't think, even if I had my hair bleached, that I would resemble that girl in any way,' she laughs.

Later, when she's under the drier, rollers perched here and there on her scalp, the hairdresser hands her an unwanted magazine. 'Twenty tips on how to lead him to the altar!' promises one article, and she can't help but read on, equally fascinated and repulsed. One of the very first tips advises her to act as a mirror, so that the man she is trying to catch sees his best qualities reflected in her. Inadvertently, she glances at her mirror image with the helmet encasing her head, its electrical leads connecting it, and her, to the plug socket. She is altered into half woman, half metal dome, like a victim in a science fiction film.

The next day in the department her hair still feels unnatural, and she has to resist the urge to keep touching it. Make sure that it is still part of her.

She's sitting next to the newest student, both of them sipping tea, and she's aware of how similar their movements are. The male fly orientates himself to the female. This is the first stage. If the female moves away, the male follows. But does the female want the male to follow her, or not? She's not sure if she's being too anthropomorphic in using words like 'want'. She admits this while staring into the cup, at the small puddle of lukewarm tea. The student clears his throat. 'We can only measure what we observe,' he says. She knows he wants to sound supportive, but she doesn't feel particularly reassured.

The tape deck has arrived in the lab and been set up with the metronome; everything is ready to go. She will spend the week watching and recording the first group of flies, then she will repeat the entire experiment with a different group.

'Different?' says the newest student. She is already thinking of him as her ideal reader, as the person she has in mind when she's explaining what she is doing and why she's doing it.

'Altered,' she stirs her tea, 'yellow flies.'

'Yellow...' he stirs his tea. It is almost a game between them, his repetition of what she says, as if he is learning by rote. She finds herself watching him, the way he moves. Afterwards she wonders what she is doing. Is this a scientific study? Or something else?

'Yellow.' She nods, thinking of her mutated flies, seemingly alike in every way to the other ones apart from a yellow cast to their body. Now she will be able to test if this one mutation will influence the way they behave.

According to the magazine articles, she did succeed in 'catching' a man. Charlie, the chap who took her out during the summer of '46, just after he'd been demobbed.

When he first phones her, she's already arranged to go to a meeting at the London Zoological Society and so she declines. He phones again a few days afterwards. Only much later does it occur to her that her earlier refusal might have been interpreted as a deliberate tactic, approved by the magazines. *Don't appear too keen! Let him do the running, that will make him feel he's in control.* This time she agrees and they go to the pictures. It's pleasant, uneventful and she thinks nothing more of it. But he phones again, and it becomes a habit to meet him on a Saturday afternoon, spend time with him that she might equally have spent by herself with similar effect. Relaxing, undemanding.

A trip to the Natural History Museum is her idea. They stand beneath jigsaw puzzles of ancient bones, stare into audiences of glass eyes. When they reach the insect rooms, she pulls out wooden drawers of beetles and flies. A stag beetle, monumental with splayed antlers, delights her. Charlie looks at his watch, 'A bite to eat? I know a café just round the corner.' But he is patient. He waits while she insists on looking at just one more array of scarabs shining up at her.

In the café he plays with the salt cellar. Chaps like him, he tells her, want to get on with their lives now that the war's over. They want to forget all about it. He doesn't explain what he means by 'it' and she doesn't ask. Instead, she watches him tip the salt over, grains cascading into a miniature mountain.

The courtship of the yellow flies tends not to be as successful as that of the wild-type flies; they are less likely to copulate. This is brand-new knowledge about the world, revealed by her and the flies. A single genetic mutation influences an important behaviour. She would like to thank the flies, she feels privileged to watch every aspect of their lives. By contrast, her own life seems somewhat less eventful. What does she do of interest to any possible observer? Shop, cook her meals, clean her digs, go to the cinema, listen to the wireless, read books from the library. She is not complaining about any of it, her routine fits her well. But the flies are the only uncommon aspect.

'What film did you go to see this weekend?' asks the newest student. 'Have you finished reading *Middlemarch* yet? Did you listen to that Prom I told you about, on the Third Programme? Wasn't it stirring?' He is standing some distance from her and now he looks away from her, out of the window of the common room, 'I should like to take you to a concert.'

She regards her hands, clean and scrubbed, the fingernails cut suitably short for lab work. Not, *would you like to go with me*. But, *I should like to take you*. She understands that he's trying something out, a phrase he's not sure about. Rehearsing it. She wonders what he expects her to do in response. They remain in silence. It's actually quite peaceful and she doesn't feel the need to say anything.

When it's time to leave the common room and go back to her flies, he still hasn't turned back from his scrutiny of the world outside.

One evening she and Charlie get caught in a sudden downpour and dash into one of the second-hand bookshops opposite the British Museum. They descend into the basement and stand dripping near shelves labelled 'Classics'.

Charlie starts to speak, more hesitantly than usual: 'What would you say –' he pauses. Horrified, she watches him retrieve a small square box from his pocket and set it on the nearest shelf.

'What would you say...' he falls silent. The box sits in front of several uniformly bound volumes with Greek letters on their spines. She thinks of all the ancient wars described in those books, as well as all the bombs that have fallen on this city and have yet to explode, still biding their time below the surface. The velvet surface of the box looks soft and inviting to the touch but she knows that to open it would be a mistake, would be interpreted as acquiescence. She keeps her hands safe in her raincoat pockets.

'I want – ' she tries to explain, 'I *need* to go back to university. I was at Oxford before, remember? I told you about it.' The box is still there in front of her. *Take it away!* she wants to shout.

'I thought you wanted this,' he says, and she feels slightly ashamed by his directness. During their trips to the cinema and picnics on Hampstead Heath, he has held her hand and kissed her, and she has let him, not realising that for him this is just the first stage. Perhaps she kissed him back. Now, trying to think about exactly what she did, she can't quite recall whether she ever actually initiated the kissing. The shame deepens; it is more connected with the lack of memory than of the act itself. It just wasn't that important. For her, he's nothing more than a pleasant chap-shaped diversion, while she makes plans to move from London to Oxford and get on with her own life.

'I thought any woman would – ' he sounds puzzled.

'But I have to go back.'

'Back where?'

Her supervisor is slowly running one finger down her tables of numbers, touching each of them in turn. 'Very good. But this isn't conclusive, you know. You have more work to do, to prove an actual link between the yellow mutation and the altered behaviour. Have you considered the role of the female?'

She's always considering the role of the female.

'The female may respond to some aspect of the yellow males. Give off a secret signal we've not yet spotted. Her reaction may in turn disrupt those males' attempts at mating. More work, Miss Bastock!'

The newest student is already in the lab when she arrives the next morning, and apparently hard at work making notes in his lab book. She peers closer. He's doodling flowers. She laughs.

'I'd like to help,' he says. 'Make myself useful, if I can.'

'I don't need help.' Everything is just as she left it and today she will record how the females and yellow males interact with each other. She has it all planned. She fetches the metronome and places it on the bench between her and the newest student. He reaches out and unclips the pendulum, setting it in motion.

'What interval of time is it measuring?' he asks.

'One and a half seconds. Look, are you here because you really want to learn from me, or just because you'd like to be associated with a successful experiment?'

His head moves back and forth with the metronome as if he's mesmerised. She laughs again.

'What do you want?' she asks. But he doesn't reply and so she indicates where he should sit, so that he keeps out of the way while she gets on with her work.

What the Theory Worries About

The theory has just been discovered, which is marvellous and a cause for celebration. But the theory is anxious because it's been discovered by a woman, and it knows (of course it knows, it's part of the eternal truth of the universe) that consequently it will be forgotten for quite a few years. The theory is about symmetry, about space. It's written in the language of cosmic time rather than human lifespans, so the theory can afford to hang around and get rediscovered at a later date. It's not urgent. But even so, the theory would quite like to be known now so it could be taught to students, written up in textbooks, argued about at conferences. Even be the subject of a Brian Cox documentary. The theory thinks that would be cool.

The theory is confident that it can predict experimental data, the sort that needs really large and expensive instruments buried underground or launched into outer space. But the theory knows in order for that to happen, a lot of people need to read the paper about it written by the woman. So far, only three people have read the paper and none of them were paying enough attention to it.

When the theory is rediscovered, it knows it will be required to pretend that it's brand new, and do the same sort of ta-da! revelation that it has already done once as it emerged from pages of mathematical symbols, as it slipped out so neatly and logically because the woman had been working so hard. Week after week she spent on the theory, while she attended departmental meetings and managed to ignore her colleagues arguing about what colour to paint the common room and whom they should invite to give the annual guest lecture.

The theory hopes that when it's rediscovered by a man, he should realise that it already exists. That he's embarrassed when he finds it in the obscure paper he neglected to read.

The theory would like it to be known that it wants to be named after the woman and not the man, and if there are any Nobel Prizes to be had, that the woman should be included. Thank you.

A GUIDE TO OBSERVING THE DEATH OF A STAR

Thank you for indicating that you are interested in learning more about supernovae, those stars that have reached the end of their lives and subsequently explode. It is hoped that you will find the following information useful.

Bear in mind that when you look at the dying star, you will only see a small part of its total light output, because a supernova emits invisible radiation at all wavelengths from X-rays to radio. This emission lasts for a few months before fading away and revealing the remains of the star, now irretrievably shrunken and diminished by its experience.

Observing a supernova is a silent encounter, like watching an act of violence on mute. Because of the vacuum in outer space, you will not hear any sonic boom or thunder-like rolls. But you will not be able to stop imagining sound waves rippling out from the star's death throes, as you look at the cascades of light in the night sky right above your head.

If you turn your attention to the constellation of Centaurus, you may be able to find shattered remnants of the first ever documented supernova, observed by Chinese astronomers in 185 CE and named the 'guest star' because it appeared in a region of the sky that up until then had been perfectly blank. This guest star was apparently so bright that it could even be seen in broad daylight. There is no firm record of what exactly happened to the astronomers themselves after they reported their observations. It was conjectured that they were imprisoned, but this might have been a rumour started by rival astronomers. Yes, bones were found in caves near their observatory, but the official records say nothing.

As you watch a supernova, an accompanying hum might start inside your skull, preventing you from sleeping when you finally stop observing the sky and go to bed at dawn. You will lie awake thinking that the neighbours' washing machine is stuck on spin cycle. Then, a day or two later, you will probably notice that you are missing out on what your colleagues are saying when everyone gathers around the coffee machine at work. Take care you do not become paranoid, it is highly unlikely that they are talking about you.

The noise in your head will wax and wane like the moon in the sky, but less predictably: an almost imperceptibly thin crescent one day, a fully rounded many-octaved blast the next. Nobody else can hear your noise, perhaps it is the audiobook version of your thoughts and feelings. Try to suggest this analogy when you get a doctor's appointment, they may find it useful in understanding what you are experiencing.

Concentrate on what the doctor is saying and under no circumstances should you mention the supernovae. Neither should you say anything about the Chinese astronomers who saw that first supernova and who were themselves never seen again. The disturbance in your head is just a physiological problem. Perhaps from now on your life will be attended by a constant and unasked-for internal noise – until the final silence.

You will have to come to terms with the fact that whenever you look at dead or dying stars, those terrific explosions that share the blue-violet colours of a bruise, you will hear the noise like the needle bumping around the groove at the end of a long play after the music's stopped.

I'm listening, you will tell each star, I can still hear you.

Once the men have finished eating and left the room, she gathers up the napkins to wash and iron them before the next meal. As she scrubs at the pale linen, she remembers the words that the men say to each other. *Quicksilver*, she repeats. *The salts of potassium and magnesium.* She sprinkles vinegar onto the wine stains.

Her work must be completed before the men return for their next meal, every knife and fork positioned correctly. *The nobility of certain gases is an enduring mystery*, she says as she wipes away a smear of polish. Nobody has taught her how to set a table so precisely and without any apparent means of measurement.

Once the men have arrived and taken their usual positions, she stands by the door. *Their apparent reluctance to combine with other substances still beyond our understanding*, she whispers, but quieter now that the men are within listening range. She is as invisible to them as air, as phlogiston, as hydrogen. Some of the more perceptive men have, over the years, detected a certain smell of household soap, and from this they have deduced the fact of her existence. That, and the cutlery and napkins, which cannot clean themselves.

In the future, the development of household devices will help her go about her tasks more quickly, and after stacking cutlery and plates in the dishwasher, she will write her own theory of valence electrons. She will grow brilliant blue crystals of copper sulphate and serve ready-cooked meals. But for now, the men have left the room again, and that is enough for her to be able to sit down at the table and help herself to the ripe fruit they always leave behind.

When I arrived here, this place was a whole new world for me. The sun shone so much weaker than I was used to, rendering a sky huge and pale above the rocks and mountains. I'd never been so far from home. But where was that, exactly? (An old question.) Maybe this could be home, at least for the time being.

I'd looked at it on Google Earth, of course. The first thing you do nowadays when you get offered a job the other side of the world. *What does it look like?* you ask yourself and you spy on your future home, zooming in until you hit the highest resolution; the point at which you can see offices, restaurants, cafés, apartment blocks, subway stops. Civilisation.

There was almost none of that here. Nothing other than a car park, next to a square building with a flat roof. That'd be the Visitors Centre, then, looking somewhat out of place in all the emptiness. A kids' playground and some sort of shed tucked away so that it wasn't visible from the front of the Visitors Centre. This was where I'd be living and working.

Google Earth also showed the launch pad several kilometres north, right on the coast of this country. A metal structure – presumably the gantry? – and some concrete blackened by scorch marks. It looked a fair distance away from the tourists area and there was a narrow winding road connecting the two, but no pavement or even a path. It was not somewhere you could walk to.

And nothing else at all for miles around. I wondered if anyone had ever lived here before the Mars Project had shown up. Or if the only locals had been a flock of sheep minding their own business before the rockets arrived and barbequed them all.

That first day I'd wandered around and looked at everything, including the peculiar landscape (so much browner than I expected!), as well as all the latest and most up-to-date images of Mars in the Visitors Centre (so much less red than I expected!) before I finally escaped, exhausted but too jetlagged to sleep, to a partitioned-off cubicle in the shed. The other workers called this shed a 'portakabin', a word I'd never heard before. I spent some time lying on the little bed and waiting for night before it dawned (haha) on me that there *was* no night because the sun barely set in the summer this far north, and there would be no more darkness than this greying of the light. Technically the days were only separated from each other by a sort of bureaucracy of the clock, and in fact every moment was destined to blur together with every other moment. I realised pretty soon I would have to introduce my own fake night, if for nothing else than my sanity, and so I rigged up a blanket across the portakabin window ('window'! It was a sheet of plastic.) and that did the trick. Finally I slept.

The blanket went up at 11 o'clock in the evening and came down again at 7 o'clock the next morning. The others laughed at me but I didn't care. I slept.

I got into a routine of waking up and folding away my blanket and making my breakfast in the 'kitchen' (which was a microwave, a kettle, a sink and an everlasting pile of dirty dishes), before having a wash in the Visitors Centre toilets. Management were always trying to stop us doing this but they were never on site, so what the hell.

Each evening after work I would go for a walk and think about how far away I was, and what I meant by *far away* in this context, and then I would go back to the portakabin and rig up my blanket and sleep (maybe, not always).

Is there a word for a place that provides you with shelter but isn't your home? There were plenty of times when I couldn't sleep and I would lie there watching the light eat holes through that damn blanket and trying not to listen to the others sitting around the bonfire outside, telling each other drunken stories. Or even worse, trying not to listen to two of them in the cubicle next door making the whole portakabin shake so much I might as well have been in bed with them. In those times I thought about whether there was a place I could return to after this summer would be over, and did that mean that the place-I-could-return-to was the place I could call home.

The tourists area with the Visitors Centre and the car park was surrounded by – was *defined* by – its fence. I could see it was necessary to stop people sneaking in without paying, but you try living in a place surrounded by a metal fence with only one gate that shut at 6pm sharp every day (and earlier on Sundays, they seemed to take Sundays seriously here). Me and fences didn't particularly get on.

My first job was issuing 'Mars passports'. These were kind of gimmicky but the kids loved them. I had to stand at the entrance gate right by the sign that said 'Welcome to Planet Alba™!', and after I'd greeted the visitors and told them where they could park, I gave them the patter about leaving the Earth's jurisdiction and entering outer space where international – *cosmic* – laws applied and they therefore needed a passport. And after the more gullible tourists got somewhat perturbed because they'd left their actual passports at home, I handed them this useless bit of cardboard that was destined to end up on the floor of their car (uncharitable of me, perhaps it would survive long enough to be stuck onto the kids' bedroom wall alongside the glow-in-the-dark stars we sold in the shop).

I could tell it never occurred to any of them to think about the admin needed to set up an actual space colony. All the officials that would have to be employed and all the boring laws and tedious regulations they'd have to implement. Someone, somewhere, must have thought about it but not our tourists, and why should they? They were paying good money to escape from the dullsville of their own real lives, to come here – even if just for a day – to experience something truly out of this world!

That's what we promised them.

So, after they'd parked their cars and entered the Visitors Centre, they had to choose between the cheaper and more prosaic exhibition on 'Mars Today™', or the more expensive, and by implication more exciting, VR suite where they could experience 'Mars Tomorrow™'. Or, given that they'd driven all this way, at least a hundred kilometres from the nearest half-decent hotel, and wanted to make the most of it, they usually (with only a little gentle sales patter) chose the Combined Ticket allowing them to find out about 'Mars Today™ and Tomorrow™'! Because that was really the best value option for them, and spending as much time as possible inside the Visitors Centre was a chance to get out of the ever-present wind, mist and rain for a decent chunk of the day. That was what they were actually paying for – an escape from their surroundings.

The display in the Visitors Centre was most impressive and, on the surface of it, quite thorough. That first day I timed myself and it took me over two hours to read all the information boards. And yet I spotted some gaps. For example, there was hardly any mention of the first Scottish spaceport (just a brief sentence or two), although at the back of the car park I did stumble across a memorial to it, where the names of the dead were already covered over with moss that was stubborn and resisted my attempts to pick it off.

The other workers separated into individual people and acquired names. It was Tosh and Little Suze who made noises together in the next-door cubicle in the portakabin. Big Suze and McFadyan (I bet even his mother called him that) talked about LiDAR and RADAR and other technical stuff I knew nothing about. 'Big' and 'Little' confused me at first because the two of them were pretty similarly sized, until Big Suze explained to me that she was a planetary geologist and interested in the formation of volcanos, mountains and canyons, and that Little Suze was an exo-biologist who studied microbes and bacteria.

Before I arrived, they'd all developed a habit of building a bonfire each night, and after a couple of days in the Scottish summer the idea of something as stone-aged as trying to get warm around a pile of damp wood began to appeal to me. So I joined them outside and I'd watch them as they gazed into the flickering flames. I was good at watching locals – the people who didn't have to think about where they came from. I've always been fascinated by that sort of person.

Sometimes they asked me questions about my life, but not always, so it was generally manageable. They kept offering me their cans of beer even though I kept declining them. 'I don't drink alcohol,' I explained but this upset them, especially Tosh, and they seemed to live in hope that I'd accept the next one.

As they chatted, the flames flickered in front of the sky still twilit in the northwest. Tosh saw me staring at it, 'Never really gets dark in midsummer,' he said. 'But just imagine being here in winter!'

'I thought this place shut down in winter, right?'

'Depends what you mean. The Visitors Centre does, the launch pad doesn't.'

There hadn't been any launches since I arrived, and I was beginning to doubt that any rockets were actually launched from this place. It seemed too improbable that anyone would want to lug rockets all the way to the top of Scotland, especially after the disaster of the first spaceport.

'The rockets get transported here by boat from Shanghai,' Tosh told me. 'Easier that way.'

I nodded, imagining the journey each rocket would take, over the sea from south to north.

'Where are you from, my friend?' He annoyed me with all this 'my friend' crap; he probably thought it was how I talked when I wasn't speaking English, so I just smiled vaguely and refused to reply. He paused to swig from his can, but he wasn't going to give up, 'Do they have rockets in your home country?'

'Tosh, I live in the United States!' and the two women laughed (as I'd guessed they would), and his question and my careful non-answer retreated safely into the landscape for another night.

After a bit, I was taken off the duties at the entrance and started work in the VR suite. This was going to be my actual job here; the first days handing out passports were apparently just a test of something or other. My inability to run away, maybe.

Now I was responsible for instructing the tourists on how to get into their VR suits and headsets. We had different sizes for adults and kids, and I had to work out the most appropriate size while explaining to all the larger people that there was a reason why the suits were close-fitting, and as soon as they clambered into them and put on their headsets nobody else would see how they really looked, because in the VR world they were represented as avatars who happened to be extremely heroic-looking astronauts. That always reassured them. They never realised that because I wasn't wearing a headset I would still be able to see them. Even as I was talking to them they kind of forgot about me, and as soon as they put on the headsets they were utterly immersed in this new world.

Once they were in their outfits and I turned on the VR display, all I had to do was watch them. You couldn't really tell one person from the other (of course you could tell the adults from the kids but that was the only distinction), they were all just people. Just humans on a new planet.

And you could watch as everything fell away from them. All the annoyances about the long drive north to this place, and the bickering between the parents, and the kids mucking around in the back seat of the car and the staggering expense of the tickets to this place, they all disappeared. It was beautiful and I loved it. I knew that if they were really there (on the actual planet and not on Mars Tomorrow™), they'd be arguing with each other about which crater to explore and how to set up camp and whose flag to fly and so on. And pretty soon it would just turn into the equivalent of one long tedious car journey. But this was a fantasy and I got to experience it every day.

I soon realised that it was Tosh who called Big Suze 'Big Suze', and he mainly did so when he was drinking, and so I started calling her 'Susan' to emphasise to her just how respectful I was and, by implication, how different to him. Anyway, by accident or (I'll admit it) design, the two of us often found ourselves (when the compound had closed to the outside world) in the weird little amusement park for the really small kids who couldn't cope with the VR suite and who couldn't read the signs in the exhibition. Susan would cram herself into a swing, and I'd push her back and forth while she hung her head right back so that all she could see was the evening sky and she laughed and shrieked. I liked doing that for her. And when I helped her out of the wooden seat afterwards, she'd still be laughing and claiming she felt dizzy and hanging onto my arm. I liked that a lot.

Of course, the reason we were busy was the first human mission to Mars. The Shenzhou spacecraft had set off from the Jiuquan launch site shortly before I came here. That was what brought so many tourists to our Visitors Centre, because this place had succeeded in getting one of only four non-Chinese licences to operate a tourist attraction directly connected to that mission. I didn't know how the Scottish Government had done it, but Susan told me it had something to do with Chinese students being given cheap tuition at the Scottish universities when the English and American ones were now off-limits to them, unless they could fork out the millions of yuan needed to get past the immigration paywalls. And the Chinese and Scottish spoke different versions of English that were apparently just about intelligible to each other. Actually, according to Susan, many of the lecturers at her university in Edinburgh were also Chinese, and the real issue was not whether anyone could or couldn't speak English but how fluent they were in Mandarin.

The spacecraft was still near the beginning of its seven-month journey but this was long enough for the media coverage to settle down into a routine stream of information about the astronauts, their backgrounds, their families, their previous jobs. Each day we'd show a 'live' data stream from the astronauts in which they'd tell us how they were getting on, and the tourists would crowd around the large screen in the centre of the Visitors Centre and watch. They loved it. And – even more exciting for them – they were allowed to record messages here to be transmitted up to the astronauts. McFadyan was responsible for vetting these messages (Management didn't want anything negative or critical being sent to the astronauts, which was understandable when you thought about it) and also for overseeing the automated translation into Mandarin.

The data feeds for the VR suite came from three rovers which had already landed on Mars some years beforehand and were busy crawling around preparing the location chosen for the astronauts' landing. But one day we got an email from Management informing us that one of the rovers had stopped transmitting, and they gave us wording to update the relevant part of the exhibition.

'It jumped off the edge of a canyon,' Tosh said when we had gathered around the bonfire that evening.

' "Jumped"?' Little Suze raised an eyebrow, 'Isn't that a bit anthropomorphic?'

'Alright, it was pushed.'

I laughed.

'What *do* you work on at home?' Tosh was at it again with his questions.

'Oh, give it a rest, Tosh,' Susan murmured, 'you don't usually care about grown-up stuff like people's jobs.'

'I work on stars. How the light generated inside them spends such a long time making its way to the surface, and how it's altered during that process.' My boring, too-technical answer did the trick: Tosh yawned and turned back to his beer. And he was on the other side of the bonfire so he couldn't see me and Susan smiling at each other.

It was Susan who showed me the gap in the fence at the back of the compound, and it was her – not me! – who suggested one evening that the two of us go for a walk because there was something she wanted to show me.

I didn't know where the others were. Perhaps Tosh and Little Suze were already docked together like two compatible bits of spacecraft, and presumably McFadyan was playing some game (he was obsessed with retro stuff like Tetris). Anyway, they weren't anywhere to be seen as Susan and I carefully wriggled through the gap until we were out in the open. Behind us, the Visitors Centre, the car park, the kids' rides, the portakabin. In front of us, the mountains, the moors, the evening light. A peculiarly sweet smell to the air.

'The whins,' said Susan. 'They're gorse bushes,' she explained, 'they always remind me of the coconut ice that my Nana used to make,' and even though I had absolutely no idea what she was talking about, I nodded.

We started to walk along a rough path presumably made by other, earlier, inhabitants of this place. She didn't tell me where she was taking me, and she didn't have a map. She must have known this place well. We walked on and on, and the light was slowly waning and the insects were appalling. Great clouds of them, delighted at finding human flesh so far from the compound, but I didn't want to complain in case she changed her mind and turned back.

We were crossing a moor and going almost due north, and I was wondering how we hadn't reached the sea yet. Although the path was reasonably flat, it was still hard going and I was only wearing trainers. I was increasingly aware of the effort it was taking to keep up with her, but I couldn't let myself fall behind. On she walked, just in front of me (the path was too narrow for the two of us to go side by side) so I could gaze at the back of her neck, which she kept slapping in an attempt to scare off the insects. Off to the southeast was a distant wind farm, its slowly spinning turbines catching the low sunlight so that they flashed messages across the land: I – WANT – YOU – I – WANT – YOU – I – WANT – YOU – I –

She stopped and waited for me to catch up, and then we looked at the view together. 'It's beautiful,' I said. I was aware this was a test of some kind and this seemed to me to be the most obvious way of passing it. Local woman shows foreign man the geographical features of her land. Foreign man praises these features. Local woman and foreign man fall in love, and live happily together ever after in a third country where they can both legally emigrate to.

The view was unnerving, to be honest. I was reminded of something and it took quite a few moments of standing there before I realised what it was. It was all so blank. No people, no houses, nothing, and only the makeshift path and the distant turbines to remind us of civilisation. It wasn't altogether different to the images of Mars.

'Did you grow up near here?' I asked. It seemed a reasonable question to me; she obviously knew this place well enough to walk across a seemingly bare and featureless moor without any sort of aid.

But she frowned, 'No of course not. Nobody lives here now.' She looked cross, for some reason, 'Perhaps we'd better go back.'

'Please,' I said, 'I'm sorry.' I had no idea what I was apologising for.

She smiled, another one of those secretive little smiles that only I noticed. (I knew I might be kidding myself about this, but what the hell. It could be a *holiday romance*, I thought.) I was close enough to see the glimmering wind turbines reflected in her lovely dark eyes.

'I can see electromagnetic radiation emitted by renewable energy devices reflected in your pupils,' I said and she laughed and, finally, we kissed.

On the walk back to the compound, she again led the way, 'Where *are* you from? You don't have to tell me if you don't want to.'

I brushed an insect off the back of her neck so lightly I doubted she felt my touch on her skin, 'I told you. America. DC.' And I was glad she couldn't see my face.

Such a long-ago journey to Washington, and barely remembered now except for a single static image of clouds from the plane's window as we flew from east to west. From noon to sunrise, we were flying back in time and perhaps this meant we could start again. Through the oval window, the clouds visible far beneath us with the half-lit new day's sky behind them, reminding me that this really was the surface of a planet. Sometimes it's easy, too easy, to forget.

During the astronauts' daily vlog we watched them bobbing around inside their spacecraft like dumplings in simmering soup. They said they were keen to show us around their new home, and they kept using this word 'home' as if they'd been practising it a lot. We saw their sleeping cabins and their bathroom, and they described in detail how they went to the toilet. We saw them preparing and eating breakfast, and I wouldn't have been surprised if one of them had put on an apron and talked about 'doing the dishes'. Apart from the lack of gravity, it didn't look that much different from our portakabin; small and cramped, and somehow insistently and grubbily domesticated as if to make the point that all you needed to be human – *wherever* you happened to be in the universe – was a microwave and some seriously horrible-looking food, much like the stuff that was delivered to us from a distant and never-visited supermarket. (We ate a lot of instant noodly things that summer.) The astronauts didn't show us the view outside the spacecraft; perhaps they were bored of it already.

'It's just stars and that,' said Tosh. 'it's gonnae look the same as from here.' Little Suze shouted at him and told him he was a philistine, and he appealed to me, 'You know about stars, don't you, Ali Baba? Won't they look the same?'

Yes, I told him, the stars were too distant to change their appearance. Only the sun would look a bit smaller and dimmer as the astronauts travelled further away from it, 'And don't ever call me that again or I'll pour all your fucking beer down the drain.'

Tosh just laughed as if he found me really amusing.

It rained a lot and we couldn't sit in the portakabin watching crap movies every evening, so we decided to use the VR suite. By now, I was working in it most days but I'd still never put on a headset, never experienced Mars Tomorrow™ myself.

'VR virgin, eh? We'll soon sort that!' Tosh, of course.

'It'll be great,' Susan squeezed my arm.

McFadyan looked worried too, 'I get seasick real easy.'

'Chrissakes, you lot are about as up for it as a busload of pensioners on their way to a funeral,' Tosh was already in his suit while the rest of us were still struggling with the various zips, 'and turn off the avatar option, I don't want to see youse making pricks of yourselves in spacesuits.'

It was my job to choose the data feed, and I loaded up some footage from the Elysium quadrangle, taken quite recently from one of the rovers (but not the one that had committed suicide). We all put on the headsets, making sure we fit them to our faces so that nothing from the outside world could impinge upon our experience.

I was alone on a planet and everything was shades of red. The dust on the ground a deep rust, the sky paler and pinker. I was scared to move my head, scared of what else I would see, and I was very aware of my own too-fast breathing and the blood drumming loud in my ears. No other noise. All around, the planet waited for me to make the first move, and I could tell it was wary.

'I come here in peace,' I whispered.

'Yeah, right,' said Mars, 'heard that one before.'

I couldn't climb the mountains or abseil down the canyons because the rovers' exploration was limited to ground level, and if you tried to deviate from this, the display simply went black. I'd warned countless tourists about this.

There was some tech feature that allowed information to be overlaid on the data feed so that as well as gazing at mountains and canyons on Mars, you could simultaneously read little squares of text floating next to them. I knew this, of course, but had forgotten about it until a box appeared in front of me telling me that the long trench I could glimpse in the distance was one that had been observed by the Italian astronomer Schiaparelli in 1877, and that, furthermore, his discovery had been mistakenly assumed to be evidence for 'canals' on Mars, dug by intelligent aliens. The box hovered and then faded away. Wherever I looked, a new box appeared. I was amazed at how much was already known about this place. The rovers had been coming here for decades, but I'd somehow still assumed it was an empty landscape. Now I saw it was already covered with words and numbers and human ideas.

I was standing there, trying to peer through a text box about a distant volcano to the volcano itself, when I realised that the others were all around me and I glanced around but of course I couldn't see them. They were in my head, moving with me. We were together even though we were invisible to each other. The thought calmed me and I took a step forward. My first step on Mars, and as I moved, the environment swayed and settled down again to wait and see what I would do next.

I had to tell myself this planet was an artefact.

Or perhaps it was me who was an artefact, who wasn't real. Perhaps the real me was outside looking through the drizzle at the summer-dim sky and pushing Susan on the swing, with the planet invisible behind clouds. And even when you could see it outside, the real Mars was a small dot in the night sky, surrounded by black, and so far away.

I felt a prickling of the skin on the back of my neck; someone was behind me, and I turned around, but of course there was nobody. Another view of distant mountains. Nearby rocky outcrops. And everything tinged red, the colour of clothing when it's been bloodied in a fight and not washed properly.

And then it got *really* weird. My vision started to focus in on something small on the ground, even though I was still standing up and hadn't moved. The rover had obviously found something that had interested it, some sort of unusual rock (I didn't know anything about geology, Earth or Martian) and had zoomed in on it.

These parts of the data feed should have been filtered out of the tourist experience; only the space scientists were interested in close-up shots of pebbles. It must have been a glitch. But it was a bizarre experience to stand there motionless while my eyes seemed to be getting closer to the ground until my head was no more than a few centimetres above it. I felt like Alice in Wonderland when she shrinks to nothing.

I had no idea how long we'd spent on Mars. The headset blocked all noise from the suite; any chatter or computer sounds were silenced. I knew that at the end of the session the screen would simply come up with the Planet Alba™ logo, which was the invitation for people to remove their headsets and come back to Earth. I'd watched them do this so many times, their faces still registering something of the sheer and utter strangeness of what they'd seen, until this gradually fell away like water and their normal lives settled back on them.

And then I realised – this experience was just realisation after realisation – that the planet was not seeing us as humans but as machines. Whilst we were on the planet, we were embodied as the rovers which had made these observations and captured these images. And as long as I stayed here, I would continue to be a machine. Mechanical diggers and glass lenses and a metal carapace. And tracks

– I knew the rovers had caterpillar tracks just like the ones on military tanks, except smaller. The same sort of tanks I'd seen years ago the other side of the fence. The tanks that I'd thrown stones at, along with all the other kids (and some of the grown-ups) in the camp. The tanks that had threatened us by their very presence.

Day after day we had watched the tanks; sometimes they were immobile, other times they suddenly and for no obvious reason accelerated towards us, and even though we were on the other side of the fence, we scattered. It is hard to stand your ground when a large machine thunders towards you. And even though the rovers were smaller than tanks, I didn't care to be embodied as one. Sometimes your future self loops back to your past and there's nothing you can do about it, and other times you can decline. Standing on Mars, being reminded of past tanks and all the accompanying deaths, I declined to be a machine.

I wrenched off the headset, but the change from gazing at a pebble on Mars to standing in a carpeted room in northern Scotland was too abrupt and I staggered and fell over. Around me the others were still standing, still rapt. I watched them, knowing they couldn't see me, and trying to concentrate on my immediate surroundings. Trying to bring myself back from memories of metal fences and military rockets lighting the night sky with fake stars. My breathing slowed. The hot and fusty room accepted me, as I found a chair and slumped on it, and changed from being a machine back to a human.

It was interesting, looking at the others. Normally, you can't watch someone else that close without them being aware and becoming self-conscious. But Susan and Little Suze and Tosh and McFadyan were on the surface of a planet millions of kilometres away from me. I sat as the four of them made tentative steps across this new world. Even after their time was up and they removed their headsets, they were too high on their experience to notice that I was already back on Earth and had been here for some time.

One evening a week or so later, we were going through our ritual of building the fire in the spot now permanently marked by soot and ash. It was easy to imagine satellites overhead detecting the flames, perhaps even detecting our faces flickering with reflected light. As the wood burnt away, Susan lightly touched my hand every now and then, and I fell into a sort of contented daze. Until Tosh spoke.

'Hey, Ali Baba.'

I blinked at him, 'I've told you before. Please use my real name.'

He shrugged, 'A nickname is a sign of acceptance, my friend.'

I stood up and left the circle, ignoring Susan's murmurs. The sky was still light enough to go for a walk, so I wriggled through the hole in the fence and went north towards the sun and the invisible launch pad that felt more and more like a myth, something not-quite-real that we told each other. I was walking too quickly over the rough ground, tripping on the tufts and slipping into the dips and hollows, jarring my bones. Still I walked further than ever before, until I could see the sea and in front of it, some way off, a structure made of metal that looked like a scaffolding tower. The rocket gantry.

Of course it was behind a fence, the same sort of fence that encircled the Visitors Centre, and this one had no gaps in it. I stood and looked at the distant tower and imagined the rockets fit snug alongside, imagined their launches and the brilliant light and noise and smoke rolling across this land.

I wasn't an astronaut trying to gain scientific knowledge of my new world, I just wanted to experience everything I could about this place, to let the land jolt me. When I first arrived here I couldn't believe the lack of trees. Here you could see quite clearly the very roll and tilt of the ground itself with hardly anything to distract you. Susan said she liked this; she could point to all the features and tell you what they were and how they'd formed millions of years ago. She didn't seem so interested in more recent history, to her 'recent' meant Mesozoic.

The gantry looked superimposed, alien. Apparently the workers who prepared each launch only stayed for a few weeks, living offshore on the same ship that carried the rocket here. The presence of the tower and fence and the corresponding absence of people were eerie.

I bowed my head at the tower, and turned back to the Visitors Centre. After I'd been walking for a kilometre or so, I noticed something else. A pale presence in the midst of the scrubby low-lying bushes. I approached it and encountered the skeleton of a sheep, its ribs and vertebrae twisted around on the grass. A jawbone, still with large square teeth. An empty eye socket. And nearby was a mound of old stones so covered in thick green moss that they merged with the ground – this moss was the most effective camouflage I'd ever seen. The stones looked like they'd once had a reason to be there, but that reason had long been taken away from them. I stood there for some time considering them. A prehistoric settlement? The remains of a sheep pen? I couldn't work it out. The place wasn't marked on the old paper map, which didn't show anything at all in this location. Neither did my phone.

'What are you doing here?' I said out loud to the skeleton. Nobody, not even Tosh, asked each other this. The wind sighed around me, and after a bit I continued to the Visitors Centre.

Only Susan was still by the fire. She held my gaze as I moved towards her and without either of us speaking she stood up and led me inside the building. We made our way to the VR suite. I chose a data feed from an area called Eden but I wasn't thinking of any sort of obvious symbolism. Still silent, we climbed out of our ordinary clothes and into our suits.

Now we were on Mars and entering Eden, which proved to be a flat plain, its ground cracked into small squares like a planetary chessboard. It was easy to walk on this ground. Well, of course it was, we were actually walking across the shabby carpet of the VR suite. We were side by side, but invisible to each other. I felt her take my hand, and now the two of us were walking together. Soon the discreet warning sign flashed up in the headset reminding us we'd reached the real-life boundary.

We stopped. We turned to face each other but we couldn't see each other, we could only look into the distance at the mountains and the two small moons in the Martian sky. And we kissed. She pulled me closer and touched me and I could see nothing of her body as we started to make love. It was like making love to the air, to the clouds. To something with no weight, with no history. We were in Eden and loving each other.

This is how it will always be for us, I thought.

We went back there regularly, of course. There wasn't really anywhere else for us to go. I was far too inhibited to do it in the portakabin, where the others were within listening range. At least we managed to turn off the text boxes so that we didn't have to make love surrounded by geological information, although Susan admitted that would be quite a turn-on for her. But we always made love on Mars; we could never just lie down on the dirty carpet of the VR suite, we reclined on the dust of a far-away planet.

Although I never explained it to Susan, what we did on Mars was a denial of being embodied as a rover-tank.

And because we couldn't see, we could use our other senses to know each other on this planet. A few weeks later, as I sat waiting in the airport for my return flight, I walked through a mist of some nameless perfume being sprayed into the air of the duty-free shop and thought of her sweet coconut smell.

Management sent a patch to correct the colour balance of the VR footage. There'd been complaints, apparently. Some of the tourists' feedback had said that the footage seemed washed out, the sky was faded and the landscape wasn't as red as they expected. So I ran the patch and was astonished by the results because now everything was almost cartoon-like, bright blue sky, bright red rocks. It didn't look real.

'None of it's real, is it?' Tosh said. 'You think the planet actually looks like any of the data they send us?' he was scornful. 'It's all made up, all tinkered with.'

'Even the astronauts?' McFadyan sounded worried.

'Especially the astronauts,' Tosh yawned, 'don't be so trusting.'

'Have you ever actually met Management?' I asked and the others shook their heads. Nobody met Management. Management were not meetable. Although they had never (to our knowledge) actually been here, they seemed to know an awful lot about what happened. One time when Little Suze took pity on a family who'd shown up on the wrong day when their pre-booked tickets were no longer valid, and she let them in anyway, we each received an email from Management saying that if this happened again we'd have to pay for the relevant tickets out of our own wages.

Management cared about every aspect of the Visitors Centre, apart from how we actually lived in the run-down porta-kabin. Our lives were sort of too small for them to notice.

In the VR suite with Susan, and I wanted to explore our new world together. I suggested to her that we could go beyond the edge of the VR data but she said no.

'Please,' I said.

'Why do you want to?' she frowned.

'Because you shouldn't be subject to stupid rules when you're exploring a brave new world.' I took her hand. I had spent so much of my life being boxed in. Padlocking the gate behind the last of the tourists each evening never stopped bugging me.

'But they haven't mapped the rest of the planet,' she said slowly as if I was thick. 'We don't have any information beyond the edge. It's there for a reason.'

'No it's not,' I was getting annoyed. 'Anyway, what about the gap in the fence? You're quite OK about that, aren't you?'

'That's because there's a real world beyond that.'

'There is on Mars, too.'

'No.'

So I took her to the mound of stones. I led her there, proud of myself for making this discovery, and I thought she might be interested in something so old. But she didn't like it.

'I don't want to stay here,' she whispered as I showed her the piles of mossy stones. Perhaps she was whispering because she didn't want the land itself to hear, to be marked by her words. 'It's wrong.' And maybe she was right. Now I saw it through her eyes, I thought that the stones were a monument to entropy, a gradual surrender to a long decay. In contrast, the sheep skeleton's twisted vertebrae looked like they were still capable of moving. I reached for her, but she shook her head.

'This place was cleared,' she was still talking in a whisper as we walked away.

'Cleared?' I didn't understand.

'There used to be farms, communities. People.'

'What happened to them?'

She turned to me, 'It's all just a beautiful landscape for you, isn't it? Beautiful and empty.'

'What happened, Susan?'

'An empty landscape sitting here, waiting for rocket launches.'

It was the very next day she told me she was leaving, and I couldn't help connecting this decision with the mossy stones. But she'd already decided to leave, she told me, it was nothing to do with that. She had only been planning to work here for a month or so, and in fact she'd stayed on longer because of me.

I didn't believe this, but at least she had the decency to tell me on the equinox, that day when everyone in the world, no matter where they are, experiences the same amount of light. I was thankful that she gave me the illusion of feeling equal to her, however briefly.

'We'll always have the VR suite,' she added, and although I laughed along with her, I was secretly upset. The two of us had been in Eden, not in some stale room in the Visitors Centre.

Later I watched her car drive away on the only road out of here, metal and glass glinting in the sun, until it turned a bend and I couldn't see it anymore, and could only imagine the long journey south towards the city. She'd told me this city was on a wide river in the west of the country and that she'd grown up there, her family moving from the countryside to work on the ships. But there were no more ships, she'd said. Now, as I stood on the side of the road, I realised she'd never told me where exactly they'd moved from.

Perhaps that was why she'd not asked me much about my own movements.

McFadyan was having problems with the software that translated the tourists' messages for the astronauts. It had been set up for English and the other major European languages (we had a surprising number of Dutch tourists), but the only English it could recognise was a 'standard' textbook sort, and many of the tourists didn't speak that. Neither did McFadyan who could be heard cursing and swearing, using words I'd never heard before now.

'What's *bawbag* mean?' I asked, but Tosh just laughed and grabbed his crotch.

Initially McFadyan simply cut out the parts of the tourists' messages that couldn't be translated, but eventually he got more inventive and started substituting other words and phrases. One day the astronauts were sent a clip of a young boy standing in the recording suite at the Visitors Centre, holding his mother's hand and saying 'The rocket's pandemonium gate will shortly be recalibrated. Do not pass go. Do not collect one hundred pounds.'

After that, he got fired. The same week Little Suze was offered work at a seaweed farm, and they wanted her to start straight away. There was one last night during which I seriously worried she and Tosh might overturn the portakabin and I had to stuff cotton wool into my ears, and then the next morning she pinched my cheek and was gone.

Tosh sat staring into his mug of coffee.

Only us two left now.

Shit.

But when he glanced up, I saw that he was crying. Tears kept slipping down his cheeks as I scrubbed at the caked-on gunk in the microwave and talked loudly about building a bonfire that evening.

'Aye,' he said finally, 'you do that, Man from Mars. You do that.'

Later, as we hunkered down in front of a small sputtering pile of twigs and he swigged from his ever-present can of beer and I sipped my tea, he warmed to his theme. 'You're from the desert, right? You've got a thing about not wasting water, right?' (I was surprised he'd noticed me turning off the taps when the others let them gush extravagantly.) 'You're always trying to pretend you know what we're talking about when really, you haven't a clue, right?'

I nodded.

'It's obvious. You're one o they friendly aliens,' He patted my shoulder, 'visiting Earth to be tempted by our women.'

'Something like that, Tosh.'

'Something like that, aye. I hope it's been worth it. You gonnae teach me some of your alien-speak, then?'

So I taught him the Arabic for 'planet' and 'orbit' and 'spacecraft', and the next morning he was gone, and I was the last one left.

I took to visiting Mars each night, choosing segments of data feed recorded during the Martian nights, so that the planet itself was quite invisible. As I stretched out on the planet's surface, all I could see was darkness and the two moons moving so much faster than our own moon, they practically whizzed around the Martian sky. If you can feel nostalgia for an experience you've never actually had, I would say that I was nostalgic for my life on Mars.

I supposed I was waiting for the astronauts to arrive, so I could welcome them. I supposed I wanted to be the first, for a change. To be the one who wasn't always a newcomer.

The expert in pain

Because her hand hurts at odd moments of the day and night, she has been invited to the hospital where she tells the doctors that the pain starts when she is peeling potatoes, or writing, or just thinking without even moving her hand. She demonstrates to them how still she can be and yet suffer. They pick up her hand in theirs and press their own fingers against hers, wanting to find the pain, or the answer to it, hidden inside her.

When did she first become aware of it, they ask, but who can ever know this? She tries to explain that it has emerged gradually from a state of not-pain, like a young girl finding out about the world. Her words don't help them understand so they decide to take an X-ray. They position her hand flat on the metal plate before leaving the room, abandoning her to the radiation.

When the X-ray is displayed, its most definite feature is a horizontal strip across her ring finger. She has never worn a wedding ring but the doctors aren't surprised; it happens at random, they tell her, on maybe one in a thousand X-rays of women, although they can't yet predict it in advance. They're conducting a study, they tell her, so they can investigate this phenomenon in more detail. They insist on showing her hundreds of X-rays of hands, all with the same black line at right angles to the finger bone – like a word on a page being crossed out, before they say they would be happy to include her X-ray in their study. Nobody has mentioned the pain for some time and she realises that they have lost interest in it. So she says goodbye, and puts her hand in her coat pocket to shelter it from the world outside.

FOOTNOTES TO A SCIENTIFIC PAPER CONCERNING THE POSSIBLE DETECTION OF A NEUTRINO[1]

2   3

4   5   6

7

---

1   An invisible partner to sunlight, a secret sharer of daytime.

2   Can a particle be said to haunt the lab equipment? I imagined the green line on the screen flickering upwards, the meter's needle trembling away from zero, the chambered mist condensing into a track. But I was kidding myself.

3   I was as invisible to the neutrino as it was to me. In its frame of reference I was nothing more than interference.

4   My ongoing failure a cause of deep anxiety for me, only alleviated by reading Pontecorvo's papers.

5   I met him once. A crowded bar where activists were known to gather, their wine casting red shadows, and the man who could explain to me how a neutrino is capable of changing identity.

6   I still have these diagrams he drew on scraps of paper. Diagrams of the sun and processes hidden deep in its core. If the neutrino has enough mass, he told me, then it can flip from one state to another, dodging the apparatus set up to capture it.

7   For me Pontecorvo was a bringer of hope. His theory a reason to renew my searches and plan more experiments. In the chatter of the bar, I had to lean towards him to detect what he was saying.

8 9   10   11

                          12

                                              13

8 According to the authorities, his meeting with me was the last one before he dropped
   out of sight. Hidden for many years until he made a reappearance in the Soviet Union.
9 Spotted in photos of the May Day parades behind the tanks and the rockets, and
   standing near Brezhnev. Just one face amongst many, but when the authorities showed
   me these photos I recognised him, because I am trained to look for all the patterns that
   light can make.
10 Pontecorvo's announcement to the entire world he is not a spy, just committed to his
   ideology. And that his name is no longer Pontecorvo.
11 This ambulance-blue flash, this link between the neutrino and nuclear activity
   submerged deep in bunkers – the authorities made me aware of it. I was naïve, I'll
   admit. Worse than naïve, they say.
12 It helps to keep my eyes closed so I can look at the darkness within. Examine it for
   signs.
13 Work on experiments will be resumed in the near future, assuming the psychological
   problems can be overcome.

The first and last expeditions to Antarctica

We were sitting facing the window with the full glare of the afternoon sunlight in our faces. No doubt this was intentional, so that we – the all-female junior scientists – were facing the all-male senior managers, who were completely silhouetted by the sun, their shadowed expressions impossible to decipher.

They were, unfortunately, quite audible. 'How can it possibly work?' one of them asked the most predictable question of all, 'How can men and women share such cramped quarters for so long, and in the most isolated place on the planet? I foresee all sorts of problems. Inappropriate relationships, competition for the women, heightened emotions, jealousy, tantrums, any number of distractions from work...' As his voice tailed off, someone else took over: 'Not to mention the problem of bathrooms!'

As the men talked on, adding to their list of imaginary problems with our proposal, we gazed beyond them at the sea. The Organisation's headquarters at Bremerhaven was right on the harbour, and the moored boats could be seen rolling to and fro in the ever-present wind. With difficulty we dragged our attention back to the men; we smiled competently and politely, we smoothed our neatly ironed blouses over our arms and we waited. With the men, we'd learnt that it was always a good idea to wait, until – like the storms that frequently occurred outside – they'd blow themselves out and nothing remained but a sort of exhausted calm.

'So you see, it's impossible!' the director announced. 'We can't build a completely separate ladies' quarters there. The cost would be enormous, and not warrant what seems to me to be a gimmick!'

Our smiles faltered at this; we didn't care for our carefully thought-through plan to work at our country's scientific base in the Antarctic to be described in this way. But we were used to this argument: many of us had heard it before. Lise's first application for a job as marine chemist had also been turned down on the basis of there being no suitable bathroom on the research boat. So had her second and third. On her fourth it was decided by someone (she never found out who) that one of the men's bathrooms could be designated as a women's simply by hanging a new sign over the old one. Thus are revolutions made. Beate's manager sidelined her, gave her the most tedious tasks in the lab until he realised that her measurement errors were smaller than other people's and her work rate higher. Now she was head of the lab. My application to become a geophysicist was initially declined because I was young and therefore had the potential to get pregnant, which would render me useless, scientifically speaking. But I just kept apply-ing, each time obviously unburdened with babies, until they gave in. So, we were used to leaping, scrambling and climbing over hurdles. It was what we did.

Obviously the director felt there could be no comeback from his last objection because he started gathering his papers together. 'Now, ladies, if you'll excuse me.' He'd already half-risen from his chair, and the other men were following him when one of us said, as if it had only just dawned on her, 'Actually, there is another possibility.'

The shadowed men stopped moving, and for a moment all we could hear was the metallic chattering of the boat masts outside.

'It's quite simple, really,' Lise continued, 'the team that over-winters needs to have experience in meteorology, medicine, seismology, atmospheric chemistry... doesn't it?' she invited the men to agree before continuing. 'Look again at our proposal. Look at our range of skills and experience. We've got a senior meteorologist from the Met Office, and one of the best atmospheric chemists in the country, as well as a seismologist with extensive experience of difficult terrains. We've got a medical doctor who's worked in the Himalayas. We cover all of the disciplines. We don't actually need anyone else, we can do everything ourselves.' She didn't say 'we don't need *men*'; that phrase had been discussed by us and rejected. It had been thought better to avoid an outright confrontation. For this was what we'd also learnt; sometimes you don't have to jump over a problem, sometimes it's enough to sidle your way around it.

Silence thickened inside the boardroom as the men glanced at each other. 'You'll do it all yourselves? None of you has any experience of the Antarctic!'

'As well as the Himalayas, some of us have worked in the remotest parts of Greenland, spending weeks hiking on glaciers. And we'll be overlapping with the current team for two weeks. We've already demonstrated that we can learn fast.' We gestured at our proposal which summarised our impressive careers.

The head of the Board drummed his fingers almost absent-mindedly on the stack of papers we had provided. 'Ladies, could you wait outside for a moment?'

The sea glittered with promise, inviting us on a long voyage, and we felt impatient, eager to get on with it, wanting to turn our backs on the Organisation, on the staid and boring city huddled on the coast, on the entire country that was always trying to stop us. We wanted to set sail.

We only had to wait five minutes before the door to the boardroom was opened again. We practised our smiles of acceptance, predicting that we were about to win. And, as usual, we were correct.

Neumayer, 1st October 1989

When we first arrived, setting foot on the iced-over steps of the plane, the men who had been here for more than a year were surprised. 'We didn't believe Bremerhaven,' they said with a frankness that would make us roll our eyes afterwards, 'We thought they were just pulling our leg when they told us about you.'

Our proposal had included an estimate of how much less food we would need than the usual all-male teams, arguing that fewer supplies would need to be transported to the base and correspondingly less fuel needed, all of this saving the Organisation an appreciable amount of money. But now the men glanced at our boxes with disapproval. 'Brought your hairdryers and make-up with you?'

Over dinner on their last night, traditionally a celebratory meal, they wanted to talk about life back home. 'What's going on?' they asked. 'We've heard about demonstrations in the east. In Leipzig, around that church. Is it serious?'

We shook our heads; there had been so much to do to get ready we hadn't had time to sit down and watch the news or read a paper. In any case, these weren't the first demonstrations in the east, and all that could be hoped for was that they would remain peaceful and nobody would be shot.

'Not interested in politics?' they commented. 'How typical.' So when they finally departed the next morning, we didn't bother waving goodbye at the plane as it dwindled to a speck in the ever-pale Antarctic summer sky. Now was our time, the moment when we realised we were a community of nine women several hundred kilometres from all the other national bases. We were the most remote group of women in the world and as we stood on the packed ice runway listening to the blessed silence, we realised we wouldn't have to meet any men for over a year, that we wouldn't have to go through the tiresome processes of dissembling, of persuading, of pretending.

We walked through each metal shipping container that constituted the rooms of the base, claiming the space for ourselves. As we did so, we removed all traces of the men: abandoned socks, cigarette packets, empty beer bottles. In the communal living space, a stack of pornographic videos had been left on the coffee table – as if to make a point. There we also found a small framed picture hung low on one wall, almost but not quite out of sight. A black-and-white photograph of men in uniform, standing around amidst the eternal snow, and when we squinted carefully, we could just make out swastikas on their uniforms. All that remained of the Third Reich's mission to this place, a failed attempt to slide an iron hook into a hitherto-innocent continent. One of us took the picture off the wall and hid it. There was no point throwing it away; at the end of our stay here we were going to have to collect all our rubbish and remove it. Everything that happened here had to be taken home, sooner or later.

We reminded each other that we would be required to do some hard physical work in intensely cold conditions, shovelling snow to be melted for our drinkwater and trekking outside every day in all conditions to inspect the weather station, and that it would be advisable to stretch our bodies on a regular basis so that our muscles wouldn't cramp. We demonstrated some yoga exercises to each other and then we went to our bunks and fell asleep. The next day some of us noticed for the first time the way the sun appeared appreciably higher in the sky than when we first arrived, but there were tasks to be getting on with and routines to be established, and thus time passed.

As a matter of courtesy, and also for safety reasons, we were required to communicate by radio with various other bases. The radio sat in its own cubicle, like a phone box in a busy street, and one of us entered this quasi-private space and manipulated the dials to and fro until she connected with another base. I think the first one we established contact with was Halley, the British base. They were obviously surprised to hear a woman's voice but politely, if a little curtly, welcomed us to Antarctica and wished us well. We decided to take it in turns to contact the other bases. The only one we did not contact was marked with a red cross by its name: the GDR's Georg Forster base right on the other side of the continent. We had been forbidden from contacting them in all but the direst emergencies.

Later, when the others were busy with their new tasks, I entered the cubicle and looked at the frequency ID for Georg Forster. But I left the dials untouched.

Georg Forster, 3rd October 1989

When the men returned to the Antarctic, everything was the same as it had been before, and it felt like travelling back in time. Even the eggshell-blue sky was just how they remembered it, and they slotted easily into half-forgotten routines; friendships made in ice seemed to be more durable than those back home, less susceptible to change and decay.

That first day they wandered through the base, reminding themselves where the essential supplies were kept: balls of string, rubber bands, candles, tins of paraffin. They discovered all the things that needed fixing; the carburettor on the main snow plough was faulty, inner doors had come loose, the weather station was more precarious on its column than it should have been. But because they had all been stationed there before, there were various procedures that could be skipped. The meteorologist didn't have to train anyone else to help him with the three-hourly weather observations, they already knew how to recognise different types of clouds and estimate the degree of cloud cover with an error of no more than 10%. Everyone knew the drills for different emergencies: loss of power, fire, accident. They practised bandaging each other's limbs and diagnosing heart attacks and stroke, and then they sat around the table and discussed the minor improvements they'd been asked by the management to make to the base. There were always things to discuss. If they concentrated on their immediate surroundings, they did not have to mention what was going on back home. And two kilometres away were the Soviet and Indian bases, where anyone was welcome to drop in and share a beer.

There was even time, between the never-ending chores, to simply stand outside and watch the sun slide around the basin of the sky. Soon the year would become a perpetual drawn-out day, with nothing but self-imposed routines to divide one slot of time from the next.

One of them, the man whose hobby was hunting for meteorites, would go and stare at the ground for long periods of time. He told the rest of them that it was possible to spot even quite small meteorites that had fallen to the ground from outer space by their essential alienness, they were dark specks on the otherwise pale land. During his last tour of duty he had found one here, quite by accident, and could not stop himself from always scanning the landscape, hoping to spot more. The Antarctic was one of the best places in the world to find meteorites, he said, because there was nothing else here.

In the corner of the communal living quarter sat the radio, a squat black box trailing wires and sprouting antennae. Daily reports were made to the management by the meteorologist, a man who had the ability to tune the radio to the right frequency, and find amidst the electric howls and shrieks a small allocation of stillness and quiet.

Neumayer, 10th October 1989

Each morning we stood in a circle and held hands and reminded ourselves that we were an unbreakable team. Then we stretched our arms upwards to the pale blue sky and that made us feel invincible before we went about our tasks and duties.

Before we left, we had been trained to look after the equipment, so that we could continue the long-standing monitoring of gases in the atmosphere, as well as seismic movements below the ice. Things went wrong all the time, of course, that was only to be expected in this environment. That was why we were there, to fix instruments that broke down or iced over or simply seized up in the cold.

Every day we launched a met balloon, and even as we watched it sail up and away, we felt it was still tethered to us – not by any physical or visible mooring, but by the information it sent; we were connected by numbers. Perhaps that was the purest form of communication possible here on this continent. We came to know this place through the measurements we made of the sky above us and the earth beneath us, and the land itself assumed a sort of purely physical significance that had an innocence associated with it.

Not long after we arrived, the catch on the weather station broke and we had to improvise a solution with a bent teaspoon and we described this small success in our letters home, letters that would have to remain here as long as we were here. Likewise, we imagined our families writing to us, and we predicted what they might say. We knew from previous expeditions that it was too easy to imagine everyone back home in suspended motion, and that when we would return a year or so from now, time would have actually jumped forward like the glitch on a tape. Nieces would announce that they no longer believed in angels, and nephews would scorn their formerly favourite games.

And in spite of all our instruments here, and all the sensitive measurements we could make of changes in wind speed, gas proportions and earth tremors, we had no way of predicting the changes back home.

Georg Forster, 20th October 1989

'What's going on in your country?' the Soviet geophysicist asked. It was evening, the meteorological observations had just been completed; the cloud cover had been zero all day.

The Soviet was sipping a glass of tea, and outside the low sun made blue shadows across the level land. They had rigged up a samovar: a coffee pot strapped to a miniature kerosene stove and complete with homemade faucet. They prided themselves on being able to do things like that.

Now they looked at each other.

'Come on, guys! You can talk to me. I heard something about Leipzig. Crowds of people every Monday evening. Apparently the church is involved.'

'Leipzig,' repeated the chemist and he glanced at the radio.

The Soviet saw the glance, 'That thing's not even turned on. They can't hear you.' He sipped his tea, 'Is it just in Leipzig, or is it more widespread?'

The meteorite hunter, who came from Dresden, nodded. The others looked at him. 'Magdeburg too,' said the chemist. And 'Karl-Marx-Stadt,' added the geologist.

'So, we can safely assume every city in your country…' and the Soviet spread his hands out wide.

The meteorite hunter was afraid to look at the others. There was a probability he had to endlessly estimate in his head; if he were not at home in Dresden, then either his family were safer or they were more at risk, he could not decide which was the correct deduction. He had assumed that they might be safer because nobody would take an interest in them, nobody would bother reporting on their daily and decidedly unpolitical to-ings and fro-ings. They might simply be unnoticed. But now these weekly demonstrations; he could not decide how they affected this probability. Would his teenage daughter be tempted to join in? And wear her purple jeans that she had acquired from somewhere (he didn't dare ask where), jeans so bright they made her easy to identify from some distance? He glanced up and saw the chemist staring at him, as if he too was making the same sort of calculation. Impossible to know for sure.

'I'm going to turn in,' he announced. And lay in his bunk all night worrying about what would happen if the Stasi realised that everything they thought they knew about his family was in fact a pack of lies.

Neumayer, 29th October 1989

Each evening Lise was required to give a little summary of the day's work to Bremerhaven. She spoke to a variety of managers, some of whose voices she recognised, but she was never sure in advance to whom she would be speaking, or what exactly they would ask. More than once she had been wrong-footed when they had required specific details of our lives, such as food consumption. 'I think they do it on purpose,' she said.

'Why?' we asked.

She shrugged, 'They like to feel in control, I think. It's because of them that we're here.'

'It's because of *us* that we're here!'

'Well, they know that really, and they're trying to reassert themselves. Power games.'

'That's why they want to know how many slices of cheese we eat? They seem more interested in that than in the ice cores we've made. They probably think their whole world is going to crumble apart now they've let women into their precious base.'

Lise nodded. 'They're fifteen thousand kilometres away. They're not really in control of us anymore and they know it.'

We were in control, it was what we'd worked so hard for, and yet sometimes I felt as if I didn't fit here. Everything in the base was slightly too large and unwieldly for me, a doll's house built on the wrong scale. The first problem was the seismograph. I could see it was about to run out of paper but I couldn't open the cover that was securely bolted to the base because my hands couldn't reach around the catches. The seismograph pen was writing its long story of the Earth's movements, and it felt like a small tragedy that soon the lack of paper would mean the pen would be simply doodling in empty space. I already had chilblains on my fingers acquired during the voyage south, and now they were sore from the repeated attempts to open the instrument. Instead I went to the kitchen to prepare soup for the evening meal, meaning to return later.

It was discovered, of course. Irene checked the seismograph and reported the lack of paper, and I was asked what had happened.

We were sitting in the dining area and I looked out of the window at the snow-covered landscape.

'It's fine,' said Irene. 'It's not a question of making mistakes, but what we do to recover from them. The first step is being clear about exactly what happened.'

'Yes of course,' I wanted to agree with her but I also had an urge to walk away from this place, get away into the snowy landscape.

'So what *did* happen?'

I spread out my hands, 'Look, I'm simply not strong enough to get the seismograph open, and everyone else was busy, so I went to do another task and then I forgot about it, that's all. I'm sorry.'

Irene sighed, 'That's the wrong way of looking at the problem. It's not that you're too weak, everything here is designed for men, so what you needed to do was use a wrench, to increase the torque you are applying. There are wrenches in the tool box. You do know where that is?'

I nodded, resenting her manner but not wanting to comment on it.

'Fine.' But she didn't look at me.

Georg Forster, 10th November 1989

At first they thought it was a joke. Or perhaps the management were playing tricks on them, carrying out some sort of psychological test to see how they'd respond. It might be an experiment to monitor their reaction to sudden and inexplicable change. After all, they were here to carry out numerous experiments themselves, it might simply be that for this extra experiment they were now the subjects.

Because how could it possibly be true? One day there were protests, larger protests than ever before, to be sure, but nevertheless, just people marching through the streets with homemade banners trying to avoid being arrested – and now this. People were climbing over the Wall and the Government was not stopping them. Therefore it had to be deduced that the Government wasn't able to stop them. The Wall had been simply overcome, shown to be made of nothing more than concrete and outdated ideas.

The Soviet popped in for his usual morning coffee, and the meteorite hunter passed it to him with shaking hands. 'All over, huh?' the Soviet said as he heaped precious sugar into the cup. They watched him drink. They'd been talking all night, ever since the first radio communication from back home, and now they were exhausted, unsure, confused.

'Anyone hurt or killed? Any shots been fired?' the Soviet asked.

They shook their heads. None that they'd heard of. Soldiers were simply standing back, obviously under orders not to fire. This was not like the '53 uprising that culminated with Soviet tanks and hundreds left dead on the streets. Neither was it the steady drip-drip of one or two people being shot every few months as they tried to get across the border. This was the sudden, and perhaps disastrous, thawing of a frozen regime, the torrents of meltwater now possibly threatening to drown them all.

'Remember Khrushchev's Thaw?' said the Soviet, as if reading their minds. 'How things got better – before they got worse again?' The meteorite hunter watched him drain the coffee cup and wipe his finger around the inside to collect the remains of the sugar. He thought about how he might write this, use this observation to make an inference about the Soviet's character and then wondered if he would have to do that sort of writing ever again. It had been presented to him as a scientific process, a way of viewing the world around him, and of capturing these observations 'for the benefit of society as a whole'.

'Well, those ozone proportions won't measure themselves,' said the chemist and left the room. After all that was happening, they still had to work, to monitor the sky and weather, detect the atmospheric gases, keep the base running smoothly. Whatever was changing thousands of kilometres away at home was not actually going to make any difference here – at least not for the time being.

Later, the meteorite hunter found himself at the weather station, staring at the steady rotation of the cups in the stiff breeze, with no memory of how long he'd been there. The weather station was a good half hour's walk from the base, and the three daily treks there involved an elaborate routine of dressing in layers of over-trousers, jackets, mittens, socks, balaclavas, goggles and boots. Time seemed to have skipped a beat. He examined his mittened hands, remembered writing the very first set of observations several years previously: extensive notes about his wife and daughter, about their daily routines, what they liked to eat for breakfast, the sort of cheese his wife bought. All of it utter nonsense and yet, when presented to his official contact, it gained the aura of objective knowledge.

Neumayer, 10th November 1989

We were finding it hard to process what we'd been told. Over our morning oatmeal, we had received a bulletin detailing the events of the previous day in Berlin and elsewhere all along the border, and now we sat, dumbfounded.

'What happens now?'

'We carry on.' We had to carry on, what else were we supposed to do? It didn't directly affect us. Anna said that she regretted not paying more attention to what was going on before we left, and the rest of us reminded her of all the work that had been required for this trip, the physical training, the preparation, learning the details of all the experiments that we were required to carry out. No wonder we hadn't really noticed.

'You know, I've never even been there,' Beate said, 'it's nothing to me.'

But I remembered that meeting in the board room and how we had been sat facing the sea with the land invisible behind us, Bremerhaven with its fish shops and little else, and fifty kilometres down the road stood Bremen with its post-war University, the concrete still shining with the promise of the '68 generation. Not much more than a hundred kilometres beyond Bremen snaked a border of barbed wire and machine guns and mines and blunderbusses and watchtowers all the way from the Baltic coast to Czechoslovakia. And just behind that border, within the east, lay a no-man's-land covered in sand that was carefully monitored each morning by the guards to detect the footprints of people trying to flee, before being smoothed again. It was that detail that made me saddest of all when I first learnt about it, the domestic task of raking sand co-opted by a military regime.

We had sat there at Bremerhaven with our backs to it all, never giving it a moment's thought as we carried out our own revolution.

'It's definitely something to us,' said Lise, 'we just don't know what.'

Later, we went outside to check the weather station. This wasn't a task that needed more than one person, but for some reason today there seemed to be an unspoken agreement that we would stick together in a group. We laced up our boots and checked each other's safety equipment. This was perhaps not warranted; the weather was forecast to stay settled with no snow or high winds likely in the near future, but we preferred to be over-prepared.

Exiting the base required going through a sort of air-lock, and the walls of this intermediate zone between two sets of doors were covered in printed notices instructing us in what order we were required to carry out some essential tasks, such as turning on the alarm systems. It was only on that day that I realised how explicit all these safety notices were, identifying and mediating possible dangers in large uppercase letters: HAVE YOU CHECKED THE WEATHER FORECAST? MAKE SURE YOUR TORCH BATTERIES ARE FULLY CHARGED! INFORM YOUR COLLEAGUES EXACTLY WHERE YOU ARE GOING!

'Hey,' I said, as we turned on the external fire alarms, 'remember Pugface back home?'

The others paused and looked at me, puzzled. Why was I mentioning a rather sleazy colleague in the Organisation? 'He came from the East,' I added, 'when he was a child. They walked all the way from Poland.' Then I fell silent, because that wasn't why I had remembered him. In any case, nobody replied.

Georg Forster, 11th November 1989

'We could get in touch with the other base,' the geologist suggested.

'The *other* base?' They were eating lunch and, in celebration, they were allowing themselves a beer to go with the goulash soup.

'Neumayer.'

'But we're forbidden from contacting them...'

'Well, I think that rule book has been comprehensively torn up,' said the geologist as he held his glass of beer up to the light and thought about a cousin – a very *distant* cousin as his mother always reminded him, scarcely a relative at all – they didn't know what had happened to him. No attempted escapes had been reported on the news that week in 1981, he had just disappeared. Probably caught as he was trying to cross, and imprisoned. Well, maybe now he could be found.

'You've already looked up the frequency ID, haven't you?' the meteorologist guessed, and the geologist didn't bother to dissemble.

'Why not? Look, we're on our own here. We have to decide for ourselves what is appropriate.'

'But – ' the meteorologist glanced at the radio.

'As long as we're careful,' the geologist offered.

Neumayer, 11th November 1989

As we sat down to lunch, the radio gave off its insistent chirrup. This wasn't the normal time for the other bases to get in touch. Lise got up to answer it and left the door of the cubicle open so we might hear.

'Hello? Ah! *Guten Tag!*' We glanced at each other, there was no other base that spoke German – apart from the GDR one.

'Yes, I'm Frau Doktor Lise Schmidt.' We heard her emphasising *Doktor*.

Silence. Lise's face was expressionless, '*I* am the leader of this mission. We're all women here.' Then she smiled and her voice softened, 'Thank you very much, Herr Doktor Muller, that's very kind of you.'

When the call ended she returned to the table and her cooling soup, 'They want to talk to us again this evening, have a longer chat after dinner about the events back home.'

'Is that sensible?' Irene fiddled with her spoon.

'Why not?'

'But we're not supposed to talk to them.'

'We're not *supposed* to do a lot of things, in case you haven't noticed. We're not supposed to be here at all, according to the archaic rules of the Organisation and their obsession with toilets, and yet here we are.'

'Exactly. That's why we need to tread carefully.'

'You know something? Sure enough – ' Lise gestured at the radio, 'he was surprised when he realised that there weren't any men here, and then – guess what? He congratulated us! Who else has bothered to do that?'

I was struck by something else Lise had said. 'Back home?' I repeated. But what was happening was in the GDR, not in our country.

As if I hadn't spoken, Beate said, 'And do we actually *want* to talk to them? We're doing quite nicely by ourselves without having to speak to any men.'

'We contact the other bases. We give regular reports to Bremerhaven.'

'Yes but that's all official. It's like a weather report, it follows a specific format and it's minimal. It's not chit-chat.' Beate looked around at the rest of us. 'Isn't it nice not having to spend time with men? We're not here to make friends with a bunch of East Germans.'

'We're not necessarily going to make friends with them,' said Lise. 'But just put yourselves in their boots. Everything's utterly changed for them, and they're stuck here thousands of kilometres from home, away from their families. God knows what's going through their minds.'

Georg Forster, 11th November 1989

'So the FRG men at Neumayer are in fact all women. Not a man amongst them, apparently.'

They were silent, imagining this new world. Was that how they did things there? Was that usual? Sure, there were plenty of women scientists back home but none of them had ever come here.

'And I said we'd contact them again this evening at 19:00.'

'But that's exactly when I need to contact the lab with the latest ozone measurements,' the chemist was gazing down at a sheet of paper, not looking at the geologist.

'You seriously think anyone is going to be waiting patiently in the lab for your ozone measurements while the rest of the country is dancing in the streets?'

'I do, actually. This is the longest continuous series of ozone soundings that's ever been measured anywhere in the world. This is something we – the GDR – should be proud of.'

So the chemist dialled the lab's frequency and then they waited for several minutes even though it was apparent that there was nobody at the other end, until finally he walked away from the radio, white-faced.

When they got through to Neumayer, they all crowded around the receiver to listen to the woman at the other end.

'Did you know what was going to happen?' she asked, 'Could you guess?'

'No, not really,' said the geologist, 'we were too busy preparing for this trip.'

'But did you actually go on any of the demonstrations yourselves?'

The meteorite hunter glanced away, the way he did in Dresden when confronted with something that might infringe the rules, so that he wouldn't have to witness it.

'I must remind you that this is an open frequency,' said the geologist, 'Anyone can listen in.'

They heard the woman make sounds of surprise, then, 'I see,' she said. 'How about this? Did you observe a larger than usual group of people outside in the streets, and if you did, what was your velocity relative to theirs? Was it zero?'

The geologist smiled. 'Very clever, Frau Doktor Schmidt.'

Neumayer, 11th November 1989

Lise frowned at us as she spoke into the headset, 'Do we need help? What do you mean?'

A pause.

'Advice? You want to give us advice on how to manage?' She was repeating this for our sakes, so we could all smile and roll our eyes. 'Well, we've managed so far. I think we're doing fine, thank you.'

I thought of the seismograph, of the information that I'd lost.

'Oh,' Lise looked at us again, 'You want advice *from* us? About what?'

Another pause. All I could hear was a sort of electronic whispering, as if the instrument was talking to itself.

'Advice about the West? Ok, what do you want to know?'

Later, in my bunk, I thought of the code word for Pugface and others like him. I remembered another woman whispering *handsy* to me at an Organisation social event as Pugface leered at us. *Not safe in taxis*, she added.

It was the middle of the night and I stared at the lines of grey light around the black-out blind. Pugface was on the other side of the planet, so why was I thinking about this now?

Georg Forster, 11th November 1989

'Is it safe?' The call to Neumayer had finished but the chemist was still doubtful. 'Are you sure we can trust them?'

'How do you mean?'

'They might report what we're asking to their superiors. It might be used.'

'I doubt that very much.'

'Well, we still have to be careful.'

'Of course. We've spent our entire lives being careful.'

Part of this discussion was simply to divert attention away from what was slightly unbearable; not knowing what their families were experiencing. Each of them had children at various stages of schooling. Was it too much to hope for that their children might not have to grow up constricted in the same way that they themselves had been? That their education would not be as stunted or deformed by political doctrine?

And what exactly was going on right now? Was everything still peaceful, had the regime really backed down when faced with the people – or were the first shots of a civil war being fired?

Neumayer, 15th December 1989

The main sewage pipe had frozen, and the first we knew about it was an ominous gurgling when one of us flushed a toilet and nothing else happened, the waste simply refusing to disappear.

'We can always go outside, dig holes in the snow.'

'There are *incredibly* strict laws about polluting the Antarctic!'

'Oh relax, Irene. Scott and Amundsen must have shat all the way to the Pole.'

'We're going to have to contact Bremerhaven,' Lise sounded dejected; this would be marked as a failure. When she managed to make contact, she was told that someone would reply shortly with advice. While we waited, we took it in turns to monitor the toilet until finally the radio chirruped.

'Hallo?' said Lise. 'Oh good, can you – '

'Sewage pipes are not allowed to freeze!' barked the voice at the other end before it cut off.

Georg Forster, 15th December 1989

'Girls, hold on! You'll be ok,' the chemist said. 'Make a mixture of warm salt water and pour it slowly and steadily into the latrines.'

'Salt,' the woman murmured at the other end, 'Of course. Thank you! Everything here seems to need constant vigilance to stop it from freezing up.'

'Well, we're quite good at vigilance in the GDR.'

Silence from Neumayer.

'Maybe jokes don't transmit so well on short-wave.'

'Ah, sorry! Haha!'

Neumayer, 15th February 1990

'Georg Forster want to know how they get jobs in this brave new world. How they're expected to compete against other people.'

'Well, we know about competition.' We knew what it was like to show up for a job interview and be mistaken for a secretary by the other candidates, and then be told by the interviewers that we were unsuitable before we'd even opened our mouths.

'Yes but we've grown up with this. We've had to cope with it ever since we were at school. They'll have dramatic change right in the middle of their professional lives. So they want to know how, when things do change, they'll have to compete with other people for their jobs.'

'We can't tell them that. We're not the Government.'

'No, but we can tell them about the process, the sort of language you have to be fluent in to convince people you've got "potential" and "leadership qualities", that sort of management-speak nonsense. They won't have heard anything like that.'

'They'll have to declutter their minds from the GDR equivalent, all group-think and talk of comrades...'

'Tell them that when you fail in the West, you're taught to blame yourself. That you internalise the system, until you're not sure where the system ends and you start.' The others looked at me, surprised. I hadn't planned to speak, but now I carried on: 'At least they have such a clearly terrible social structure that they can point to it and say that is the regime's doing, we're surviving in spite of it and it's nothing to do with us.'

'I'm not sure that's true,' said Lise. 'I think they do internalise it, and participate in it, just as we do in ours.'

I faltered. 'Maybe. Just tell them it won't be their fault, even though they'll be made to feel inadequate.'

Lise sighed, 'Speaking of which, it's time to give the daily bulletin to Bremerhaven.'

Georg Forster, 30th April 1990

The chemist was able to chat briefly with his wife over the radio when she visited the lab back in Berlin, and afterwards he told the others, 'She's been shopping on Ku'damm!

Went to KaDeWe and bought some eau de cologne. Says you absolutely would not believe the prices, and they all think they're being ripped off by the West Germans left right and centre.'

The meteorite hunter hadn't spoken to his wife, and wasn't sure if he wanted to. He was afraid. At night he thought of all those documents detailing so many months and years of mundane events; meetings with neighbours, chats with colleagues, visits from his daughter's schoolfriends and their parents, his wife's complaints about her colleagues. He had always provided so much information, and most of it fictional. There had to be too much of it for anyone to actually read. And nothing had ever happened to the people he'd written about, he was sure about that.

If he hadn't done it, someone else would have. That was why he did it, to keep his family safe from the indignity, the intrusion, the danger of someone else spying on them. He hoped that in the future this would be understood. By whom, he did not know and would not speculate.

Neumayer, 15th May 1990

It was not long before the Antarctic midwinter, and time itself seemed frozen into a persistent cycle of chores, both individual and collective. There was no weekend here, no change to the routine, we never had a single day off. The weather station had to be recorded, the met balloons released, the atmospheric gases measured, the seismograph monitored, the snow melted, the food cooked, the base kept as clean as we could manage. The only aspects of our lives that didn't follow such a set routine were our conversations with each other and our chats with Georg Forster. All other communications remained formal. It was Lise who mostly talked to Bremerhaven; as well as being mission leader, she had more patience, and perhaps more experience, than the rest of us in dealing with that sort of management.

After the first few months, when they had been asking us all sorts of bizarre details about our food intake, Bremerhaven seemed to have settled down into a – not quite courteous, but at least predictable – relationship. Until this evening, when Lise seemed to be taking longer than usual to give her daily bulletin. Several minutes after she started the call, we could see her frowning. 'What? Sorry, why on earth do you want to know that?'

A pause.

'I've no idea. I'll have to check with the others and get back to you on that. You say you want this for scientific purposes? It won't be used for any other reason?'

I noticed that her cheeks were faintly flushed.

'I see.'

When the call was finished, she came back to the table and without any preamble she announced, 'Bremerhaven are interested in our menstrual cycles.'

'What!'

'They want to know how we're coping in the extreme conditions, and if our cycles are syncing. You know, groups of women are supposed to sync when they live together.'

'Tell them to mind their own damned business!'

'Well, it's not a surprise. They did ask us to take pregnancy tests before we left. It's not that different. And perhaps it would be genuinely useful to know how women cope with periods in this sort of situation.'

'The same way we cope with them everywhere else! And we refused the pregnancy tests! Honestly, Lise, you didn't *agree* with them?'

'But you can't deny it's a scientific question.'

'I think it's the same old shit we have to put up with all the time. And how exactly would you report it? Are you going to start each bulletin by giving them a list of who's on the rag?'

Lise was staring down at the table top, 'I'd anonymise it, of course.'

'Well, that makes it just dandy!' Beate stormed out of the living quarters and back to her bunk, where we could hear her banging around.

'We can't help interacting with our surroundings. If we monitor those surroundings, it makes sense to monitor ourselves too, and our response to this place. It's an ecological approach.' Lise was still trying to justify her response to Bremerhaven.

'Yes, there wouldn't be anything wrong with that, if we're in charge of what we're monitoring. But we're not.'

'Just give them the wrong information about us. Make something up.'

'We can't do that! That's unscientific!'

'What I've always worried about,' said Irene, 'but it's now become more obvious, is that we've come here as scientists to carry out essential experiments, but we're also being used as the subjects of other experiments.'

'And what do we do about that?'

Irene thought for a moment. 'Turn it on its head. Use *them*. Record everything they say to us, so we can write about the way that male managers seek to control female scientists, even over long distances. So that future generations will be more aware.'

Lise grinned, 'Good idea.'

'Pugface,' I said. 'He cornered me in the stationery cupboard.'

'He did that to me too,' said Irene. She looked at me, 'Maybe that's why they didn't want us coming here.'

'What did you do?' said Lise.

'Wrong question, Lise!' said Irene. 'It's about him, not us!'

But I wanted to reply. 'He put his hand up my skirt, and what did *I* do? I brought my own paper and pens to work so I could avoid the cupboard.' I paused, but the others remained silent, waiting for me like they did when I lagged behind them on the walk to the weather station, making sure I could catch up with them. 'They keep going on about safety here,' I continued, 'Every time you talk to Bremerhaven, they remind us about some procedure or another. But safety *here* isn't an issue for us. It's probably the safest place on the planet for us.'

Georg Forster, 3rd October 1990

They'd invited the Soviets and the Indians for a little ceremony that was due to be held later that evening, the hauling down of the old GDR flag and the raising of the new German one.

'Except it's just the same old West German flag,' said the chemist.

The geophysicist waved his hand dismissively. 'Don't carp. We've got a genuine problem.'

'Which is?'

'What are the words of the national anthem? We should sing it when we raise our new flag.'

They all thought for a moment.

'Better get on the blower to Neumayer.'

Neumayer, 3rd October 1990

'Oh dear, nobody's ever asked us that before!' Lise was laughing but she also looked embarrassed.

'Aren't you celebrating too?' the geophysicist asked.

'I suppose so. Yes, we should.'

'Anyway, we feel we should sing the national anthem and we don't know the words,' the geophysicist repeated.

'The problem is, I'm not sure we know them either.'

A puzzled silence. 'How can you not know your own country's national anthem? Didn't you have to sing it at school or in the scouts, or...' the geophysicist trailed off.

'No, not really. That's not how it works with us. In fact I don't remember ever singing it at all. It wasn't exactly a popular choice when we were growing up. But we could tell you the words to "Ninety-Nine Red Balloons", we all know that one by heart.'

Georg Forster, 3rd October 1990

The Soviets and Indians arrived and stood around, grinning and self-conscious. While everyone else was washing mugs for the Sekt, the meteorite hunter touched the thin fabric of his new country's flag and prepared to tell them about everything he'd been required to search for.

Georg Forster and Neumayer, evening, 3rd October 1990

'I'm not sure I actually want to sing,' Beate said.

We were outside in the slanted sun and the long shadows. There was an hour to go before the official ceremony in Berlin, and it was apparent that Georg Forster had been drinking celebratory Sekt for some time. Bremerhaven hadn't even mentioned the Berlin ceremony to us, so we agreed Lise would say nothing to them about how we planned to celebrate it. It would be an undocumented experience shared with Georg Forster.

'Oh come on, it's a historic occasion. Besides we've been here a full year. Let's celebrate that too.'

'Not by singing about unity and justice and freedom.'

'Aha, you *do* know the words. Why didn't you tell Georg Forster?'

'Because it's nothing to do with me. As a woman I have no country. That's why I wanted to come here, a country that nobody owns.'

'Well, why don't we have our own celebration of a year on the ice, with blocked sewage pipes, a whole bunch of new East German friends, more than a hundred successful ozone soundings and thirteen menstrual cycles.'

And so we all hummed along to the drunken singing from Georg Forster on the other side of the Antarctic continent.

Latent image

Mum told me that you had gone to live in a castle and this was her one and only answer to all my questions. I had proof of it as well, the photos of stone-grey walls with turrets edged as neat as any birthday cake. The knights in armour and their horses were out of sight, hunting beyond the castle grounds, and the outlaws hidden in the dungeons.

You'd send the photos to me by post, a fat brown envelope waiting next to my bowl at breakfast. Mum pouring tea, making sandwiches. Me, spooning up porridge and flicking through these photos. There must have been hundreds of them, all variations on the same image, like a note on a piano being played over and over again until the reason for it's been lost in time.

With Mum bustling around safely out of sight in the kitchen below, folding sheets and pairing socks, I could take out the albums and look at what you wanted me to see. You never took a single photo of her and I didn't either, not realising the need for one until it was too late.

A couple of pictures showed a thin streak of shadow that could have been caused by you. Maybe the nearest thing I had to your self-portrait. A few others had blurs smudging the castle, or pale wisps patterning the lawn. I thought they were ghosts, but Mum said they were just people, moving too fast for the camera. But I knew that this was the way you really saw them, no more than an interference of light getting in the way.

Like Mum, you're also gone now. But you're more solid and more physical than when you were alive because you rattle when I shake you, making a noise like gravel scattering on the road. It seems appropriate for you to be kept in a closed box, safer than out here in the open. Hidden.

We only went on one trip together, you and me. I would have been about nine, and you took me down to London, to see an exhibition of pictures of the Moon taken by the Apollo astronauts. Rocket landers and dust, the astronauts' faces invisible behind their helmets. And the sky blacker than anything I'd ever seen before. There's no atmosphere on the Moon, you told me, no air molecules – nothing at all to scatter the sunlight. Moon people don't see an ordinary yellow sun shining in a boring blue sky like we do here on Earth, you said, they see a perfect white disk in a perfect black sky. One the utter opposite of the other.

I remember you telling me how difficult it would have been to print such blackness. We'd expect a little bit of speckle to disrupt the perfection, you said, due to the printing process. But look closer, you told me, and you'll see that there is none. So I did look closer, ignoring all the usual things: the footprints, the helmets, the flags and so on, and I agreed with you. We stood side by side as we inspected the photos, two pale faces floating next to each other in the glossy Moon-black sky.

I have a camera too, you said, like you were revealing something to me that I didn't already know.

Now I wonder how it felt to remake the world how you wanted it to be, into a sequence of stopped images. To render all movement invisible.

Whenever they let you come home, we'd find you waiting on the doorstep with your rucksack leaning against you. Your camera hanging from your neck in one of those brown cases that was rounded at the edges, like a rock worn away by the wind and sea.

At first it would be ok, you and Mum sitting in the kitchen every morning after breakfast and going through your pills. But before long you'd pull our lives out of shape, unravelling them with your nighttime journeys through the house, like it was a new land for you to discover in darkness. You'd climb up and down the stairs and walk the length and breadth of each room, and I couldn't sleep for the sound of your endless footsteps.

It wasn't just the house itself. You'd detune the radio, transforming BBC words into amplified howls. You'd light the gas hobs just to watch the colours in the flames. You'd construct elaborate structures of fishbones around the bathroom.

One summer afternoon. Dark clouds collecting in the warm air and an excited feeling in my chest of something proper about to happen. Now. Bang. Now. Another bang. The noise and light seemed so determined, so willed, that I couldn't believe it was just random. And neither could you, because we found you under Mum's bed. Curled into a tight ball, hands clamped on your ears and screaming at the thunder.

It's all just look-at-me, Mum said later. Everything's out to get you, but only if you judge yourself important enough, she sniffed as she stood at the sink, the potato peel slipping easily from her fingers like fishing line being reeled out. Maybe she was thinking she should have made a better catch. Something better than fishbones and pills and radio static.

I hope you never judged her. She let you come back, after all, over and over again. In every version of your return, she'd sit you at the table in front of your plate of poached eggs or baked beans and keep an eye on you as you tried to angle the food onto your fork. She did you the honour of not feeding you like a baby. I'm grateful to her for that, at least.

You should have been grateful, too. She always went looking for you when you disappeared, potato knife glinting in her hand as she searched the house and garden, peering under beds and in cupboards. She'd find you in the shed and in the empty bathtub and behind the sofa. Once she found you in next door's allotment, your mouth stained berry-red, garden string wound so tight around your wrists that you wore bracelets of thin bruises for days afterwards.

The three of us sometimes managed to find our right places, you perched on the edge of the sofa, Mum settled into the easy chair, and me twisted into the velvet curtains breathing in everything they'd absorbed – the tobacco and cabbage and sweet institutionalised scent of you – while Mum talked on and on, her words as predictable as rain in school holidays. You staring at your feet as if trying to remind yourself about your own body.

I remember picking up your fishbones from where they lay in the miniature sea of the bathroom sink, and holding them next to my face. Feeling them stroke my cheeks when I should have been brushing my teeth. Your face floating above mine in the mirror, and I noticed for the first time that we looked quite alike. Our reflections giggled at each other, and I laid the fishbones down again.

Only later, when I was trying to sleep, I felt afraid. I liked the fishbones, you see, and I understood why I had to return them to exactly the same position. It was no different to Mum lining up her knives in the kitchen drawer. Bones were as important as knives, weren't they?

We could manage days, even weeks like this. But it always went too far. Fishbones would progress to meat, and then to animals. That time I found next door's rabbit in your bedside cabinet, felt its heart pitter-pattering with fright. None of us was ever surprised when things went wrong, because they always did, and you'd have to go back to the castle. A few months or a year later, you'd try again and come home, and it would go wrong again and you'd leave.

It only changed after Mum went. She'd got so weary of the sight of pills she stopped taking her own. One day I heard the washing line snap and I found her with the sheets billowing around her like a tent that had lost its moorings.

Now, I sometimes wonder how you and her happened and how I was made. She never said and I never thought to ask until after I saw her lying there, her hands clutching the still-damp laundry, as if this absence was only momentary and she'd return and slip back into her own body. I wanted to ask her everything after that, but of course I couldn't. By then you were beyond telling me anything.

Now you're gone too, and all I have are the negatives. Cardboard folders of them, sent from the castle in a box with the rest of your belongings; a dressing gown and slippers that shaped themselves to you like plaster casts. I could make a statue of your feet, if I wanted.

I ease the negatives free of their protective paper casings and hold them up to the window. When I get used to the light that's dark and the dark that's light, I realise what I'm actually looking at. This reversed castle is full of people. They crowd by the walls and stand around on the wide lawns, where I used to imagine the knights' horses lowering their beautiful, blinkered heads. The worst of it is that all these people are in focus. You kept them from me. You didn't want me to know about these people in their hospital gowns.

It's hard work looking at people the wrong way round. The only thing that's true are the walls, because grey's the opposite of itself. But the castle is so much smaller than I imagined; the vast wall that I thought was built to keep out foreign armies is in fact just the low barrier of a car park. The courtyard is forlorn with suburban flower pots, and the paving slabs are 1950s-precise.

The people – they're like you, I can tell. In love with the intricacies of fishbones and too familiar with the varieties of possible pills. As I look at them, I forget I'm looking at negatives and I think that maybe this is the way it really was for you and the rest of them in the castle, living under a black sky. All of them with a perfect whiteness to the middle of their eyes.

In one of these folders every strip of negatives shows pictures of narrow beds in narrow rooms. On the last strip of negatives is a picture of a cupboard with something long and thin snaking out of the back of it, as if it's trying to escape. Next is a picture of a bench, and I can see it's positioned by the cupboard. The very final image is a close-up of the long, thin snake, revealing it to be a coil of wire attached to a plug.

All these beds lead me to a single destination. You're showing me a sequence of events, writing me a story I don't want to read anymore. I throw the negatives onto the floor so that they scatter everywhere, and I refuse to pick them up

But I can't stop myself imagining a hundred people clipped into place on the bench, and plugged into all that mind-dazzling violence. I know there is no real reason why the doctors electrocuted people in the castle. Perhaps they thought talking wasn't scientific enough because words are so difficult to interpret, and electricity has such a simple, numbing power. Now I feel I'm the unwilling witness of something I wasn't allowed to see directly, something that took place in an inverted world beyond the lens.

There's a blank sweetness to a person who's gone, through this treatment, their mind's been remade as smooth as a hospital bed. After Mum had gone, you kept looking for her because your memory of her going must have been shocked out of you. You'd scarcely any memory of me either, and I'd almost given up hope until that one word, 'Moon'.

Moon. For that, I kept you as long as I could. Listened to tuned-out radios with you, and cooked you mackerel for tea so you could add to your bone collection. Together we looked at photos of the castle that never changed. You showed me the camera, taught me how to look through the viewfinder, adjust the focus, make a decision and click the button. We clicked right through the summer and into the autumn, accumulating canisters of exposed film.

Even the going wrong was just part of the process, and by the end of it, when you were sitting in the back of the ambulance, waiting to be taken away again, I felt your gaze brush over me as gentle as a fishbone settling against my cheek.

But without you present, I couldn't help worrying about the hidden design of your illness, waiting for it to develop in me. The only thing to do was to take control. I changed the house from the place that you knew, I installed a lino floor printed to look like real wood, artificial window shutters that don't protect the rooms from the sun and a balcony that's too meagre to take my weight. All these things pretending to be different to their true nature. You could never have done that. You could only be what you were, and so my desire for fakery is proof that I'm not succumbing to it, at least not yet.

You couldn't come back to a place you didn't recognise, so you never came back here again. And now I wait in my remade house for the illness to emerge, like an image on photographic paper becoming visible in a darkened room. I watch myself in the bathroom and I click the button on your camera. But these films will never be developed. Latent images are a promise that's broken by the developing process. As long as they stay hidden, I may stay like this.

Mrs McLean and Margaret are now in charge

Before I started work there I'd never seen anything like it, a building all curved and white like a giant mushroom and making me feel that I've shrunk to the size of a caterpillar. Inside has a peaceful feeling, similar to a church after the service has ended and everyone else has left, and it's just you and the altar flowers.

On my first day I asked the old boy who seemed to be in charge how I was supposed to clean the telescope, because I had never seen one before and I was really very unsure about tackling all those different dials and so on. Nobody back at the bureau had explained it to me, they'd just said this place was part of the university but a bit further out of town, and an easy job. Looking at that metal contraption covered in fingerprints and sorely in need of some Brasso, I wasn't so sure.

No, no, said the Old Boy. I was never to touch the telescope itself, just clean everything around it, and it was very important that I should be most particular about the dust because it interfered with their work. Their job was to look at the stars, and mine was to deal with the dirt. A fair division of labour was how he put it, and I agreed because I couldn't argue, could I?

I had to ask him where the cleaning utensils were, and he waved a hand towards the corridor. But when I found the right cupboard and tried to open the door, it was quite stuck and all seized up. I wrestled with the handle, making a bit of a racket until the Old Boy poked his head around the office door. He didn't offer to help. In my experience they never do.

Some days I find a cluster of younger men round the Old Boy. I gather he's their university teacher. It's more work for me on the days they're here but nobody else notices that. I mentioned it to the bureau, they weren't interested either.

The main room where the telescope is has a black-and-white chequered floor which always reminds me of Billy's chess set that I gave him for his fifteenth. He taught me to play so he could practice, but I didn't really see the point. Now as I swish my mop over each of the squares, I can't help thinking about all those rules that had to be learnt. I never did get the hang of it. 'Wrong move, Ma!' Billy would say as he knocked over yet another of my pieces, and Mr M would chuckle.

In the summer, I don't see a soul. I have the whole place to myself, and can sing as I work. In winter, when the days are short, the men arrive before I'm finished and they settle down to wait for sunset. They obviously don't notice me. Don't misunderstand me, they're perfectly polite when they need to be, it's just that there's nothing about me that they seem to be able to focus on. They don't tend to realise that when I'm trying to get past with a bucket full of dirty water, it would be a good idea to move out of my way, otherwise I might slop it on their shoes. I have been tempted.

I can tell when it's the Old Boy who walks on my wet floors because his footsteps are so uneven, the left stride is longer than the right. A wooden foot, probably. I notice things like that after my stint in the military hospital. An office is an office, they always say back at the bureau, and all that's required of you, Mrs M, is to do the lavs and mop and dust. But that's not true. Every job's different. It was in my very first week after I'd finished for the day and left the building, that a little oblong slit appeared in the mushroom-roof, becoming wider and wider, until I could see the telescope itself peeking out. I stood stock-still for quite a few minutes, in danger of missing my bus. Mr M would be tickled by that, I thought.

When I leave there in the winter months, I always glance back behind me so I can see the roof with its mouth open, looking like it's wanting to ask a question. I don't think the men notice me taking a peek. They never say. They never say very much to me at all even when I'm mopping around their feet. But they talk to each other about the moon and the stars as if these things were right there in the room with them.

In the afternoon they crane their necks and peer up at the sky. 'Fine weather tonight,' they'll say to each other. Or, 'Patch of cloud to the east but it'll soon pass.' Two things I have learnt from this. One is that they always say the same thing, no matter what the weather actually looks like, and the other is that they are always optimistic. Even if it's raining, they say 'Oh, it'll blow over.'

While they look at the sky and speculate about what the night's weather will bring them, it's my job to see to what's on the ground and closer to home. I dust and sweep and I mop and I remove the dead leaves that are always piling up in the entrance and I shake out the doormat. And of course I do the lav.

That first day I had a slight problem. I'd been working several hours and drunk my thermos of tea and now I needed to spend a penny. But where? Of course, there was no ladies, only a gents. I briefly considered going outside; a group of trees just behind the building would offer me shelter. When I'm walking in the Chilterns there's nothing to it, up with the skirt and take care to crouch properly so you don't water your shoes. But I couldn't do that here. What if someone saw me and complained to the bureau?

I'd already mopped the floor of the lav with Jeyes and squirted bleach into the toilet bowls and urinals and wiped the sinks and taps and topped up the paper. So I didn't want to dirty it again, but I really had no choice. As I went about it, I wondered if any woman had ever been in here before. I am a pioneer, I said to myself. Well, what about that, Mr M replied.

One day last autumn there was a bit of a commotion. I was concentrating on the floor around the base of the telescope, where there are always lots of footprints, when

I heard a shout from the office, so I dropped the mop and went to find out what was what.

It was the Old Boy. 'Oh, Mrs McLean,' and he pointed at the radiator, 'there's something over in the corner, making some sort of noise. Could you go and see?'

I recognised that sound straightaway, the tiny desperate thump of a mouse trying to free itself from a trap. I peered down the back of the radiator and discovered a miniature kingdom of spiders' webs, abandoned body parts of daddy longlegs, upside down bluebottles. I doubt anyone else had ever looked behind here, I suppose it was all somehow too small for the men to care about. If you spend your nights studying the moon or the stars, you may not have the right sort of eyes to notice the things that are under your feet.

The mouse was pinned to the trap by the metal bar, one bright black eye facing me as it clattered around the dusty floor. I bent down to get a closer look. I didn't really want to touch it but I had no choice; it deserved a quick death and it wasn't going to get one unless I took charge. Behind me the Old Boy was sighing and clearing his throat. He probably thought none of this had anything to do with him.

'I'll need a bucket of water,' I said, more for the mouse's benefit as a sort of warning of what was going to happen next, but the Old Boy sighed again. When I returned, I saw that the mouse's eye was dulling, and it was wriggling with less vigour. The Old Boy had moved away from his desk, and seemed to be inspecting the bookshelves on the other side of the room. 'I'll just drop the mouse in the bucket,' I said, louder than was needed. But the mouse's tail was problematic, too thin and whip-like, and I had to steel myself to grasp it.

After it had sunk, I counted three small bubbles that broke the surface and then nothing more. 'At least it wasn't a rat,' I commented. Silence. Just me, the bucket and the Old Boy. I glanced at his back, at the worn tweed jacket with its elbow patches, at his creased neck and shiny scalp. I waited but nothing happened, so I picked up the bucket and carried it through to the main room, where the younger men were standing around in a group, peering at some sort of chart pinned onto the wall.

'Excuse me,' I said as I worked my way past them to pour the contents down the drain. The day was bright, the bucket full of sunlight hiding the dead animal beneath the water's surface.

This autumn it's different. The air raid sirens are practising their song to lure us into the shelters, the balloons have floated high into the sky. The time for politicians waving pieces of paper is over. Each week fewer and fewer young men gather around the Old Boy, because everywhere the men are disappearing from the streets and trams and shops, the way they did the last time. War comes round like a season of the year. Like winter. Ah well, says Mr M. Let's hope they had a better time of it than I did.

The Old Boy reminds me more and more of an umbrella that's been neatly folded and propped in a corner, before being forgotten by its owner. Now he's going too. 'No students to teach so the university has no further use for me,' his smile goes as lopsided as his walk when he tells me this. It's the most he's ever said to me.

'What about me?' I say. 'Am I still needed?' Nobody at the bureau has mentioned anything. I have to ask because Billy may be off at some hush-hush establishment but there's still the rent.

'Mrs McLean, you are essential. Keep this place ship-shape until everyone returns!' He unrolls a length of blackout over the telescope itself so you can't see what it is anymore, and I think of the mouse hidden under the water. As he's putting on his mac, he tells me, 'Keep an eye out for Miss – ' and then there's a name I don't quite catch, 'she'll be popping in to keep an eye on the place every now and then.'

'Well, I'll be doing that,' I say. Doesn't need two of us for somewhere this small, but I don't say that out loud in case he agrees and I'm out of a job.

He shakes my hand, quite firmly, wishes me luck and then he's gone.

Now I'm the only one left, I mop the floor without having to worry about getting in the way of anyone. I can do the work according to my own routine. The whole place feels bigger, there is more space for me. When I finish work I've taken to sitting in the chair by the telescope. I'd like to stay here one night, I'd like to see what the men see. Why should anyone mind?

When I'm waiting at the bus stop for the bus back to Hendon Central, I glance up and almost lose my balance. Where have all these stars come from? Like the mice that venture further and further into the building (recently I've found droppings right under the telescope itself), the stars have made themselves quite at home above the darkened war-ready city.

Later I realise I've left my thermos flask behind and I'm cross, because the dregs'll be all sour and difficult to clean. But next week the flask is in the scullery, someone's rinsed it out and left it to dry. And like a clue in a detective novel (Mr M rolls his eyes when I read them but it helps me to relax), I find a hankie on the floor of the lav. Not a men's hankie: it's embroidered with tiny flowers and smells of nice perfume. I pick it up and fold it neatly and place it on the chair by the telescope, still hidden underneath the blackout fabric.

There never was a Mr McLean. Or rather there was, but I never met him. He came in useful at a time when I needed a sort of alibi because of Billy. I got his name off a war grave, which might have been bad luck but at least the poor sod couldn't complain. In return he gets to see a bit of life and the pleasure of my conversation.

She's not a cleaner, your Miss – , he says now.

No, I reply. If that nice perfume is too expensive for me, it's too expensive for any other cleaner. I can work things out, you know. I'm not daft.

Finally, I meet her. When I arrive, someone's already unlocked the door before me and I can feel that the place has lost its emptiness. There's nobody in the room with the telescope, but the door to the office is open. I hear papers being rustled and the soft clearing of a throat, so I stick my head around the door.

A young woman is sitting at the Old Boy's desk, looking at a piece of paper as if she understands what's written on it. She glances up. 'The famous Mrs McLean,' she says, quite composed but not unfriendly.

'Hello,' I say. 'How do you do?'

'I'm Margaret,' and she holds out her hand.

Later, when I've finished work I go to say goodbye. The rain's stopped, the sky looks sort of rinsed clean and I can tell that it might be a good night for whatever she wants to do here. And I'm right because now she's in the dome, peeling the blackout off the telescope. I help her with this, and we deal with it the way that two women will fold up a large bedsheet, our hands not quite meeting around the edge of the cloth.

'Are you one of the Old Boy's students?' I say this without thinking and she laughs. She's already cranked open the ceiling so we can both see out of this room and into the night.

'Here, Mrs McLean.' For the first time ever I feel bad about calling myself this and wish I could tell her my real name, but of course it's far too late for that. 'Come and listen to this.' She puts her head against the telescope so that one ear is resting on the metal itself and beckons me over.

I have never ever touched the telescope itself. Not in three years of working here and cleaning droppings and sorting out dead mice and swishing the mop around the men's feet. I'm not sure about it, it doesn't seem right, but she's quite clear what she wants me to do.

It's cold and very smooth beneath my ear and it's quivering like it's alive. Just small movements, reminding me of the mouse in its trap, until there's a sort of jolt that makes me jump back, startled. She laughs, but a bit grimly.

'It's the bombs,' she says, 'making the ground shake. When I look through it, the stars are juddering all over the place. The sky's so lovely and dark but it just won't stand still, Mrs McLean.'

The Old Boy would never have said anything like this, not to me. 'What can you do about it?'

'I don't know. I can only look at the stars on clear nights and that's when the bombing is worse. Huh!' and she laughs again, and rummages around in her handbag before producing a packet of cigarettes. 'Smoke?'

That's how the two of us end up standing side by side, our backs to the telescope that's still trembling with each new bomb. Afterwards, when she moves to the window to check the sky, I watch her walk right across that black-and-white chess board floor like she's the queen.

Unsettled

I never can remember the name of this town. 'K, it begins with a K,' that's what I would tell anyone if they asked me. We – I mean the department – moved here a few months ago. We were relocated to save money, that's the whole reason for me being here.

The windows in this building are criss-crossed with wire so that the lorries lumbering along the nearby motorway appear as pixellated as the images on the screen. Whenever my eyes get tired of staring at the screen, I press 'pause' and I blink and look away. And now, at 10:38 on a Wednesday morning somewhere in the middle of September, I stop looking at traffic and I start work again.

I'm 'IMAGE SUPPORT SECTION 1.1b'. When I started in the department, it was so long ago that we still used film photographs taken from planes. We were in charge of monitoring coastal erosion all around the country, and it was my responsibility to develop the photographs. Things have changed a lot since then. About twenty years ago the department replaced film cameras with digital ones, and more recently it replaced the planes themselves with drones. Lighter, cheaper and it doesn't matter so much if they crash. Now there's no part of this job that's the same as when I started it, but officially I've never changed jobs. I'm like the proverbial cricket bat that's had both its handle and its blade replaced. Is it the same bat? Am I the same person as I was when I stood in the red light of the dark-room watching land giving way to the sea?

The next image is a rectangle of foam-flecked water and it's not particularly interesting or noteworthy, so I'm about to press the appropriate key when I catch sight of a speck in the top right corner. I zoom in until I reach a cluster of orange pixels. Nothing this fluorescent can possibly be natural so it's obviously another piece of plastic junk. The algorithm estimates that it's taking up 1% of the whole image. I classify the image and I move on to the next one. Click and refresh.

Later that evening and I'm back at the flat watching people on my laptop. It's just some rubbish reality programme but it makes a change because I don't see many actual people (either on screen or off) at the department. Sometimes the drone's images include dog walkers on the dunes, or occasionally a camper sitting outside a tent accompanied by a wisp of smoke from a bonfire. Occasionally, four bare legs all clustered together. Just once I saw someone teetering on the edge of a cliff. I wanted to call the emergency services but it's prohibited to inform people outside the department about the content of the images. In the end I told my boss, and he replied that it was too late to do anything about what I'd seen, because it always takes a few minutes for the images to be uploaded from the drone to the system, and in those few minutes anything could have happened.

I wonder if they noticed the drone as it hovered above them, or if they were too intent on balancing. Or not balancing.

It's ten o'clock, and in the flat next door the music starts up as usual. I sip my vodka at regular intervals and I look out the window at the grass, even though it's dark now and I can't really see anything. Does it count as looking if you can't see?

I take another sip of vodka, and the sound from next door retreats just a little bit further away and the screen blurs slightly.

The next day I receive a meeting request: 'First meeting of the relocation committee at 5pm in room 3.14 – please be prompt! We have a lot of business to get through.' So I log off the system and I leave my room with plenty of time to spare. But I realise for the first time since I started working here that not all the rooms in this building are numbered sequentially, 3.10 is next door to 3.15 with nothing in between but a wilting spider plant on the window ledge. The thing's in obvious need of water, but now I'm late so I hurry past.

I poke my head around the door of someone's office to ask them where I should go, but this woman just holds up one hand as if stopping traffic and continues typing with the other. I wait until it's clear she's not going to break off from her work for me, and then I carry on down the corridor.

Room 3.21 is emitting voices and laughter, and that makes me hopeful but when I pause in the doorway, everyone falls silent and they don't start talking again until I've retreated. I check my emails while I walk, in case there's been an update and the relocation committee has been relocated itself. But, as I should know by now, the department doesn't go in for self-referential jokes, and according to my calendar the meeting is happening right now in room 3.14. Perhaps it's time to give up and go back to the flat. So, in the end that's what I do, stopping off at the corner shop where they haven't yet realised I'm a regular customer, and I buy the week's second bottle of vodka.

For me, the beauty of vodka is its transparency. It's undetectable, it won't be seen in any image. As the flat vibrates to the sound of next door's music, I hold my glass up to the evening's darkness and the grass outside and the blurred TV as if I'm making a toast to them all.

The next morning. The other beauty of vodka is its purity and I feel fine, everything is just as sharp as it needs to be.

Download (look, decide), click. That's what my job looks like in the training manual, with the human functions tucked away inside the brackets. Today I go through this sequence upwards of a hundred times before I stop for a coffee. I gaze at the lorries and briefly wonder where they've been and where they're going, and then I continue.

My boss pops up in a corner of my screen for our weekly meeting. To save bandwidth he always uses a text box, his speech blossoming out of the white space.

I tell him: I couldn't find the relocation committee meeting yesterday. Wrong room number maybe?

And he replies: You got that email by mistake. You were sent information about a meeting that was held in another building.

Why?

I'll look into it. Don't worry, those meetings are pointless window dressing. The unions wanted them, so we agreed. Yada yada. Now, update please. Anything interesting or unusual?

A never-ending glass of vodka, the unseen grass outside my flat, all the lorries that are always leaving this town.

I saw an orange object, might have been a life buoy? But then the text box freezes, the connection has broken and my boss is gone.

This morning I classify various species of seabirds in several images. Three more images contain fishing boats, and in one of those images I can't see any fishermen. They must be below deck sorting through their catch, or else they're hiding from the drone. The fishermen tend to have some odd ideas about the drones, even after the department's recent public communication exercise. Sometimes I see them shaking their fists at me. Or rather at the drone, but I'm the one who has to look at their faces. I mentioned this to my boss once, and he said if I felt upset about what I saw in the images, then I could get counselling as long as I didn't talk about the details of what I've seen. Official Secrets Act and all that. But it's precisely those details that I'd need to talk about so I've never bothered.

Lunch in the canteen. I read the newspaper and I eat chips, and I wonder about the relocation meeting. What needs to be discussed? Noisy flats, distant lorries. An orange life buoy with nobody in sight. But if a life buoy's floating in the water, it must have been used. Fishermen don't wear them, they say it tempts fate. Someone else, then. Who?

I look around the canteen. My boss could be one of these people and I'd never know because I've never met him in person. Security issues prevent that.

In the afternoon the drone sends me images of cliffs and churned-up dark sea. The images nearly all show gannets and other seabirds diving into the water and I click the same button over and over again. There's a storm building in these images, I can see it from the waves growing larger, and I can almost feel the damp wind deposit salt on my skin.

When the next image is downloaded, I realise I'm looking at a woman in the water. The drone's as low as it ever gets, and she's quite high up out of the water, so I see her head and shoulders from behind, and her long wet hair streaming down over her back, shining in the afternoon sun. She must be swimming. The drone does occasionally capture images of people swimming in the open sea, but how could she have got down into the water from the cliffs? There's no boat in this image.

I want to see the woman's face, and this is the first time for ages that I've wanted anything like that. I'd like to watch her swim, watch her slice through the water. And even though I can't see her properly, I can tell how confident she is. She's in her element.

I've been staring at the woman for so long that the system starts to clog up, and I hear a beeping sound as more and more images are downloaded but I don't deal with them. Finally I decide on the classification and I press the appropriate key. But I want to keep the woman to look at another time, so I also save the image onto my home drive. I'm not supposed to do this but the system doesn't stop me.

I carry on working. All the time she's on my mind and it occurs to me that she might have been in trouble. She didn't look in trouble though, she looked in control. But the image doesn't make sense, she can't be there. There's no way she could have got into the water from the land.

I've never saved anything onto my home drive before, it's a fairly useless part of the system. I'd like to copy her onto a memory stick and take her back to the flat with me so I can look at her on my own laptop, but we're not allowed to use memory sticks for obvious reasons. Nothing is supposed to leave the department. But I'm good at remembering images, and in the flat that night I hold the vodka up to the blue-sea light of the screen and I toast her.

Emails continue to arrive from people I left behind when I moved to K, and I should answer them, but I can't talk about what I do all day and the vodka isn't news to anyone anymore. So the emails bunch up in my inbox until I move them to the junk folder.

The next morning, my boss appears on my screen. This is an unscheduled meeting.

`Why did you save that image?`

When I don't reply immediately, more words appear: `I get a status message whenever you do anything like that.`

That's a surprise, but I suppose I've never saved anything to my home drive before. Still, I don't type.

`I know you're there. I can see you.`

Of course he can, I should have known this. I try to avoid staring directly at the little round camera at the top of my screen, and my hands hover over the keyboard until finally I come up with: `I wanted to work on that image later. Remember you told us to spend more time on the difficult ones.` And I try to appear relaxed, because I really don't have anything to hide. The reason why I wanted that image is nothing to do with work.

`Who told you to save data to your home drive? I didn't. What else you got hidden there? Daisy Duke in her birthday suit?` He knows I don't have anything like that. The department doesn't allow access to the internet. `Anyway, there's an issue with that image. Your classification appears to be incorrect.`

`Incorrect?` I'm never incorrect.

`It's been classified elsewhere and that classification isn't based on any human content.`

Who else has seen my woman? Who else has classified
it?

You're not the only one who gets these images. I
allocated the same dataset to 1.1a a few weeks ago
and so far the two of you have been in perfect
agreement, until yesterday. When one of you decided
you'd seen a mermaid.

Silence.

My hands lie motionless on the keyboard.

Well?

He's waiting for me to respond, to justify myself. But I
can't, until something occurs to me and I type: If 1.1a
agrees with me about everything else then they saw
the orange life buoy, didn't they?

And as I suspected, as soon as I finish typing this sentence,
the text box disappears and up pops the usual message
about a broken connection.

I sit there, the morning's images downloading every 30
seconds and beeping away at me. I go to my home drive,
but of course the image of the woman has gone.

I get up and leave my office and I walk down the corridor
and right out of the building. Nobody stops me. Outside,
the strong noonday sun makes me blink but I keep going. I
walk past the corner shop without stopping.

In the flat, the remainder of last night's bottle of vodka is still on the table so I put it in back in the freezer. I turn on my laptop and watch some news footage of people crammed into tiny boats on a distant sea. Then the boats have all capsized and people are thrown into the water, trying to hold their children above the waves. People crying out for help, screaming at the camera, but of course the camera does nothing. The camera never does anything. I turn down the sound but that makes it even worse. Now it's too similar to the silent images at work.

My fingers move over the keyboard. Why did I see an orange life buoy?

And as I always suspected it could on this laptop, even though it never has before now, a text box pops up.

A silent white box. I stare into the fake eye at the top of the screen and I wait until this appears: It's nothing to do with your section. Nothing to do with the department.

Yes it is. I type this immediately.

But the text box is implacable. It's nothing to do with any of us.

What does it mean by 'us'? Who is 'us'?

You know who we are.

I don't — I've never even seen you. Anyway, I gave it the wrong classification, and so did 1.1a. I want to change the classification.

It's too late for that. And the text box disappears.

I shut down the laptop.

It wasn't a piece of rubbish. I should have classified it as a person. Even though I never saw that person.

I leave the flat, walk to the station and choose a train. A small, slow one that lumbers away from K, over the motorway bypass and between the fields until it reaches the end of the line. Then I walk along a country path and I'm heading towards the sea. I know this because I can smell it. As I walk, I classify what I'm seeing. Cumulus cloud, wind turbines. I can't help it anymore. Black-faced sheep, female roe deer. I have to classify, it's automatic. Hopping ravens, clods of earth, a recently ploughed field. It's what I've been trained to do. Two magpies close enough for me to see the oily blue sheen of their black feathers. Howling wind. But you can't classify air.

Finally, I reach the cliffs and I walk right up to the end of the grass. I can hear the seals before I see them, hear the thin high-pitched noise that they sing to people like me who have a secret longing to be lured away from their homes. The seals all turn their heads towards me. Sometimes when a seal is low down in the water and only the top of its head is visible, it looks like a bird, and it's easy to mis-classify them on the drone's images. Other times a seal looks like a woman. And sometimes it doesn't look anything like a woman but you just really want it to be one.

I know that the woman in the water wasn't real. The drone created her, she only existed in the image. But I am here, teetering on a clifftop and holding my hands out to the emptiness that can't be seen by anyone else apart from me.

THE SHORTEST ROUTE ON THE MAP IS NOT THE QUICKEST

He wanted to meet in some café behind Waterloo Station. I hadn't heard of it before but clearly the cabbies liked it, because the narrow street outside was full of their taxis all parked up in neat rows, like black metal beetles waiting for the order to carry out an insect invasion of London.

We got our coffees and I started by asking him about his time in Helmand. This confused him, how relevant was it to the real problem? But you have to sidle up to these things crabwise, and it didn't take too long before he began to talk. He told me about travelling the roads in slow convoys at a precise speed, all the tanks bunched together so that nobody would get left behind. About knowing you were being watched by the enemy hunkered down just beyond the horizon and not being able to do anything about it. About seeing the road ahead all kinked through a periscope. About scanning, constantly scanning every track and inch for things that shouldn't be there.

When I considered that the time was right, I led him back from that distant place and I asked him how long he'd taken to pass the Knowledge.

'Two and a half years,' he said with pride plumping up his voice. Fair enough. Most people who attempt it, if they pass it at all, take far longer than that.

'Tell me, is there a special map that you cabbies use?'

He shook his head, 'Maps are almost useless. You start with the endpoints of each route that you have to know, say Manor House Tube to Gibson Square. That's the very first one you learn. But what if one of the streets is blocked with roadworks or an accident, or just buggered up with traffic? So you need to learn alternative routes. And the best way to do that is to go there and experience it. One foot in front of the other. Slow and steady.'

I couldn't hide my astonishment, 'You *walked* all the routes in the Knowledge? But aren't there over three hundred of them?'

He nodded. 'Well, the weather's a bit better here than in Helmand. And the walking's safer.' Then he ducked his head, 'Actually I cycled a few of the longer ones. Call me a cheat if you want.' And he grinned, so a certain shy charm that must have spent its time hidden away inside him could now be spotted breaking through the surface, before he positioned two fingers some way apart on either side of his cup. 'When you do the Knowledge, you got to learn how to negotiate around that coffee. It's large, it's hot and it's causing a hell of a traffic problem.'

I watched as he traced some imaginary routes on the Formica table. Some were graceful arcs, others irritable little detours that travelled straight up to the cup and then buckled around it at the last minute.

'The sooner you're warned about the coffee, the better state you're in. The more possibilities you have and the quicker the detour will be.' He looked like he'd solved a major problem and perhaps he had. 'City's a creature in time as well as space. A traffic jam starts on one road, soon it'll shit on the whole area. There's feedback in the system. Walking, you get to learn the correct timescales for things to pass, for everything to normalise.'

'What about GPS?' I asked.

'What about it?' He laughed. 'It'll just send you down an alley full of dustbins or stick you behind a million buses on Piccadilly.'

The second meeting. Beforehand, I'd read up about mine clearance in Helmand; what he'd told me seemed unlikely but not impossible, and I found myself looking at manhole covers in a rather different way. I was beginning to get the measure of the space between what he said and who he actually was. In cases like this it was always essential to find this space because if all I had to go on were his words, things would be difficult for both of us.

'I like to work at night,' he said, after we'd been served our coffees.

This was the first time he'd admitted to any feelings, so I made a note of it.

'In the city the night sky's the same colour as rusty old cars.' This clearly reminded him of something, 'You got a lot of abandoned vehicles on the roads and quite often they were booby-trapped.'

He was sipping his coffee rather delicately, I thought. It was easy to imagine his hands supporting the weight of a gun, fingers curved around its trigger. But I had to be careful with imagination, it had misdirected me in the past.

'You want darkness in the city at night – you look at the buildings, not the sky. Rows of black windows so regular they must be telling you a story,' and he drummed his fingers on the table. 'Of course a lot of the city just ignores the darkness. You got to get out some distance if you want real nighttime. Drive right out into the suburbs. There's a beautiful emptiness about a shuttered-up Tube station after midnight, with no-one around but dogs picking at rubbish and eyeing you up like you're an intruder on their territory. And perhaps you are. Sometimes I go out there and turn off the engine, just to sit and watch for the moment each morning when you see the land separate itself from the sky and drop back down. Then I go back home.'

'Where's your home?'

'Near Manor House Tube.'

The starting point of the Knowledge's first route. Very neat. Maybe too neat. Maybe I was being led somewhere, deliberately.

'And you lived there with – ' I left the question open for him, but he just sat there seemingly lost in the remains of the afternoon, with the café emptying out all around us and the proprietor stacking crockery in a noisy manner on the long metal counter. When he did speak, it took me by surprise.

First he tilted his cup so it could capture the sunlight, and the white china gleamed at us both. Then he told me about her: 'She worked at the university. She took me there once, and I was surprised at how small the entrance to her department was. How a place that dealt with such big questions could be tucked away like it didn't care if anyone even noticed it or not. Her office wasn't much more a cupboard and piled high with stacks of paper. So much paper, and all of it printed with these numbers and letters about the universe.' He moved the cup around while he talked. By now it was right on the edge of the table and the proprietor was hovering nearby, wanting us to pay.

On the way home I wondered about his nighttime dogs picking at rubbish. Have you ever seen that in the suburbs of London? And then I wondered about the cupboard full of paper and what exactly was being recorded there.

The third meeting took place the very next day. Again, it was quite late in the afternoon.

'The land is revealed by the light most clearly in the morning or evening, when the sun's right low down. Then you see all the bumps and hollows of the shadows. Noon is no good for anything. No information in the midday sun.'

He talked like there hadn't been a break, like he hadn't spent the previous night criss-crossing the streets of the city, driving people to where they needed to be. It was a gift he had, I could tell, to pick up where he left off. Like we were always in the present moment together. Maybe he lived his life in the present; some people did.

I wondered if he was the sort of cabbie who enjoyed talking to his fares.

'Not usually, I can oblige them if they expect it but I don't initiate. Although more and more tourists nowadays want the patter from us. It's a persona. But that's OK because it's nothing really to do with me. Leaves my mind free to wander.'

The sun shone fierce through the café windows, and the only shadow was cast by the streetlight outside, slanting a thick and dark line right across the table. He positioned his little espresso cup in this shadow like he wanted to hide it from view.

'What did she do?' I asked.

'Dark matter,' and we both almost laughed at the absurdity of it, of sitting there in a café with squeezy plastic tomatoes of ketchup on each table, talking about something called dark matter.

'When we first met,' he continued, 'she used to talk quite a lot about her work. She was trying to map some invisible stuff out there,' and he waved his hand at the grey London sky. 'Stuff that wasn't lit up with stars like a Christmas tree, that's needed to hold everything else together and stop it flying apart. Her words for it, not mine.'

'What do you think she meant by that?' I asked him, and he shrugged. 'What was in the shadows was more interesting to her. In return I told her about the city and a bit about the land too. What I'd seen and not seen.'

The sun had disappeared some time ago behind the clouds, and the espresso cup was left stranded in the flat grey light of the afternoon.

'The land? Where?'

'Here and there. Now and then.' It was then that he first told me about the bundle of rags he'd glimpsed in the distance through the periscope of the tank. The bundle was lying heaped in the middle of the road. It looked to him about the size of an animal, or a small child.

Don't stop to see what it is, they'd been commanded, and so they hadn't. The convoy had kept going at the same precise speed, approaching the bundle, neither slowing down nor speeding up. You could get used to travelling that way, he told me; it felt like you were moving through space, just floating along. Until you looked through the periscope and reminded yourself what was all around you.

Don't even swerve to avoid it, they'd been commanded. So they'd had to run right over the top of it, feeling the tank shudder like it was breathing. And the rest of the convoy had done the exact same thing. It could have been a booby trap, designed to lure them out, or make them change track into the path of the mines. Or it could have been exactly what it looked like: an abandoned body. How could they tell?

'I checked the underside of the tank afterwards, picked out a piece of rag. Nobody else in the convoy mentioned it.'

We sat in silence. The shadow had come back which was a relief; it gave me something to concentrate on.

'But someone had to know, so I told her all about it. You know what she said in reply?'

I waited.

'That not everyone believed in dark matter.'

'How long were you and her – '

A year. A year of being happy together. He was happy, at any rate. And when they reached that first anniversary, she talked to him about orbits, about planets and stars always travelling around the same fixed spots, so he had to conclude she was happy too. Then she explained that those orbits didn't actually make sense unless you knew about dark matter.

'How did you meet?'

She was a fare, of course. He picked her up at Victoria Station and she asked him to take her to her office, and then started arguing with him about whether he was really going the quickest route. She told him to go straight along Exhibition Road and then Cromwell. He was used to this argument, even as he drove her left-right, left-right through the choppy little mews streets of Knightsbridge, ignoring what she was saying.

It might just have ended there, with both of them feeling a little bit annoyed and no tip for him. But she spilt a load of papers over the seat and floor, and was still scrabbling to gather them up by the end of the journey. So he parked the cab, turned the meter off, and told her she had all the time in the world. She thanked him. He was only being polite, but then they happened to glance at each other in the rearview mirror.

'Sometimes, looking at another human in a mirror is better than face to face,' he told me. 'You notice more.' He made some gesture with his hand that I couldn't follow. And I didn't understand why she'd told him to drive that route, because it wasn't the right way at all from Victoria station. Perhaps she'd got the names of the streets wrong.

Anyway, they'd had this year together. And he'd been shown some photographs of long, thin curves of light in the dark sky. Nothing at all like normal stars, this light was all stretched out and bent. She'd seemed proud of those photos. It was only in this distorted light pattern, she told him, that you could discover the truth about the dark matter, the stuff that did the distorting, wrapping space and time up into knots. They were in bed when she told him this.

I cleared my throat, slightly embarrassed, and made a note of all this in my little book. We drank the rest of our coffee in silence. I didn't say anything because I wanted to hear him talk some more.

The proprietor took our cups away and then in a deliberate fashion also removed the napkins, the wipe-clean menus, the teaspoons, the sugar bowl, the salt and pepper shakers and finally the plastic tomato. There was nothing on the table now. He had to speak.

He spoke. There hadn't been a row or anything, but she left him. She just disappeared into thin air. She'd always kept her own flat, and so for a couple of days he assumed she was there. They didn't live in each other's pockets, he didn't own her. He said this quite vehemently as if I'd been arguing this point with him. She was her own woman.

'Did you ask at the university?'

He nodded, of course. But they wouldn't tell him anything. He'd only been to one departmental party with her so nobody knew him there. He'd asked to look at her cupboard full of paper in case there were any clues there, but that was off-limits apparently. So finally he'd gone round to her flat, and that was when things had really turned upside down, because another man had answered the door. Had leant against the doorframe, wearing nothing but a dressing gown and smoking a cigarette, listening to his frantic questions. Had said through the smoke that he didn't know anything about her. Had never even heard of her. Could have been lies, could have been the truth.

He'd hung around the flat for a bit, not doing anything, just watching, but someone must have noticed because the police arrived. He couldn't afford to get into any trouble. If he did, he'd lose his green badge and his livelihood.

There was a tiny trail of sugar crystals leading across the table that I hadn't noticed before. I made a note of the address of this flat; it was the obvious place to start. 'What colour dressing gown?' I asked.

He didn't seem surprised at this. 'Brown.' He indicated his cup. 'Coffee-coloured, I suppose. Espresso.'

He'd tried asking at the places where they used to go together, the pubs and restaurants and so on. But of course nobody had told him anything. And now he didn't know what else to do.

'So I just thought that all I could do was look around. But where to start?'

It was then that he realised. Maybe the best thing to do would be to simply let his fares decide for him. Every route would take him somewhere different, and he could keep his eyes open, scanning the landscape for her. She had to be out there, somewhere. On the street, sitting in a café, hidden in a building. She was still in the city, he was sure of it. He even felt he might have looked at her during his searches, without realising exactly where she was.

I shut my notebook. 'I'll agree there's a hidden logic to your method,' I told him, 'but it is pretty random.'

He nodded and almost smiled. That was the whole point. He'd tried the other approach, but the quickest way of working through the entire city was to travel randomly, and let other people decide for you where you should go. The fares didn't know this, of course. They didn't know that when he was driving them to their destinations he was searching, searching all the time. They didn't know what essential function they had.

'So why do you want me to look as well?' I asked him. 'If this is the perfect method, then what can I add to it?'

'I'm not sure,' he said. 'But I can't stop working, because when I'm working I'm looking for her. And if I do stop working I'm still thinking about her and me, and how it was between us.'

He fell silent. The proprietor continued sweeping the floor with rhythmic swishes of his broom, working it against each of the chair legs.

'I'm very tired. I thought that you're a neutral person, you've got no connection with either me or her, you may be able to see the pattern in all this that I can't. There's always a pattern, isn't there? An orbit.'

When he'd first told me about the dark matter, I'd thought it even more unlikely than his experiences in Helmand. Perhaps I'd doubted too much in my life. But it seemed to be real or at least, a lot of people had convinced themselves it was real without ever actually seeing it, which wasn't really the same thing at all but would have to do.

'Tell me honestly,' I said. 'Didn't the two of you ever argue?' And he looked down at the floor as if indicating to me that he could see something hidden beneath it. Behind us, the proprietor paused in his work.

A UNIVERSAL EXPLANATION OF TOAST

I've always fancied myself as a particle physicist, and this morning when I enter the common room and smell toast, I know I'm going to have my first real scientific success. The institution's assistant is already sitting at the table, and without looking up from her open newspaper, she slides the little plastic cup of pills towards me, like she does every morning. But I ignore this because I'm here to work.

The smell indicates to me that a slice of bread has recently been exposed to a short but intense burst of heat, in turn caused by electrical resistance in a current-carrying wire grid, the bread's surface correspondingly raised to the correct temperature for the melting of butter.

But there's no plate on the table, and neither is there any crockery in the sink. Or even cutlery – apart from a solitary teaspoon that, when I pick it up and hold it against the back of my hand, emits a very slight warmth, like a small star destined to end its life by being locked away in a part of the galaxy too far from public transport for any visitors to reach. Or, now I come to think of it, like the universe itself as it continues cooling, as predicted by the second law of thermodynamics. From this I can only assume that the assistant recently used the teaspoon to make herself a cup of tea, and has since drunk it and hidden the mug from me.

While I search in the bin for evidence of teabags, she continues to read her newspaper, tracing each line of the code I've never been able to crack. Although an odour of sweetened citrus permeates the room, I reject the presence of marmalade as superfluous to my deductions.

I touch the surface of the table and feel water. A damp table is one that has been wiped recently, and a table is wiped because it's dirty, and it's dirty because it's had crumbs scattered on it. From this I can deduce the existence of carbon produced by helium atoms, these atoms themselves being primordial and thus formed in the Big Bang. A slight asymmetry right at the time of the Big Bang – perhaps not dissimilar to a fault in someone's brain when they are born – has led to the universal dominance of matter over anti-matter, and a local (at least here in this institution) dominance of toast over anti-toast.

The assistant has nearly reached the bottom of the page and the end of her story, but I've got there before her. 'I've solved it,' I say, but she still won't look up, so I'm forced to raise my voice. 'I can prove it all, the existence of molecules and atoms. Quarks, leptons, bosons and the origin of mass itself!' And because she's always such a polite lady, she closes the newspaper, sighs quietly and prepares to listen to me.

An investigation into love by Babcock and Wainwright

The first time that either Babcock or Wainwright saw the mouse was just after it arrived in the lab, as part of a new delivery on a Monday morning. They had only been working there for a few months and they didn't know each other very well yet. So it was just chance that they were standing side by side next to the cage. Their research examined the mating behaviours of mice, and they were planning an ambitious new experiment.

The mouse seemed to notice them because it stopped investigating its new home and it gazed right at them. All the other mice continued to run around, messing up the clean straw and squeaking incessantly, whereas this one just sat very still. There was definitely something going on behind those black eyes as it looked from Babcock to Wainwright and back again, and they could not stop watching it. Only when it finally lowered its head did they glance at each other.

Wainwright thought he'd never seen anything so wonderful as Babcock's gentle forehead or her shiny hair. Her lab coat seemed blessed with an aura of knowledge. Babcock, in turn, gazed at Wainwright's witty nose, his thoughtful mouth and his entrancing ears. And they fell in love.

The mouse scurried away to the back of the cage.

Lab mice, if they're not dosed with something nasty or engineered to fail sooner, usually live for about a year or so. They tend to be well looked after, they're kept clean and dry, and they're fed the right sort of food on a regular basis. No cats can get in to terrorise them, and they are excused all traps.

A month after the mouse arrived, Wainwright moved into Babcock's little flat. In the mornings they would cycle to the lab and in the evenings they would cook spaghetti. At night they always curled up together, partly because the flat was cold and it was a good way of keeping warm. Occasionally Babcock went to the cinema with her friends, and when she did, Wainwright had a drink with his ex-flatmates.

Out of all the thousands of genes that made up the DNA in this mouse, just three were different to other mice. This unique combination of mutant genes was sufficient to create slightly different proteins in its body, which supported a slightly different balance of bacteria on its skin and fur. This meant that the mouse smelt a bit odd to the other mice, and as a result, they didn't like to go near it and it had to sleep alone. But every morning it sat near the front of the cage, and Babcock and Wainwright came to say hello to it before they started work. Because they were trained to notice animal behaviour, they saw that the other mice were keeping away and this worried them; perhaps the mouse would be cold at night. One day they watched as the other mice formed a sort of barricade around the food, preventing the mouse from eating. It didn't look like the type of mouse which would try to fight for its fair share. It looked too intelligent for that; it probably understood the ultimate futility of physical combat.

They discussed whether they should liberate the mouse and bring it home with them. Of course this was against all the rules, but they knew it would be happier with them and they could look after it and keep it warm and fed. So, in preparation, they bought a cage from the pet shop, and discussed how to sneak the mouse away from the lab without anyone else noticing.

However, this plan was a bit optimistic, because they were not the only ones who had been affected by the mouse. The lab technician left his wife and started seeing one of the lecturers. The cleaner embarked on a passionate affair with the other lecturer. The students all fell in love with one another, in a seething cloud of hormones even more intense than is normal for students.

Soon, everyone in the lab was in a relationship, and everyone was hanging around the mice cage, hoping for a sight of the mouse. The cleaner would pop in at lunch time for a quick look; the students liked to stroke the mouse's head. But the lab technician was not too addled by love to bawl them out one day when he caught them actually cuddling the mouse.

The only animals in the lab who did not love the mouse were the other mice. They shunned it, and it became stressed, which caused a larger than usual amount of adrenaline to flood its system, making it ill. Its nose became dry, its whiskers drooped, its eyes lacked their usual lustre and Babcock and Wainwright realised they had to act soon.

But as they crept through the lab that evening after everyone else had left, they sensed something was terribly wrong. The cage was absolutely still; the other mice were nowhere to be seen. The mouse lay on its side, partly covered by straw. It was beautiful, but it was also dead. Babcock burst into tears, and Wainwright comforted her.

The next day the lab held a wake. According to protocol, a post-mortem should have been carried out, but nobody could bear to cut into the mouse's body, so it was buried with full scientific honours, and the latest copy of *Nature* was used for a shroud. No lesser scientific journal would do.

Soon after that, Babcock and Wainwright started to write a paper about the mouse. They described how they had observed it living apart from its cage mates, and how it had died sooner than expected. They discussed a link between the other mice shunning it and its death, and possible physiological explanations. After some lengthy and heated discussions about the appropriateness of referring to their own feelings in a scientific publication, they wrote a footnote to the paper which stated, 'The authors felt a particular affinity with this mouse.' Babcock wanted to write more, but Wainwright disagreed.

When they weren't working on the paper, they stayed at home feeling sad, and in their grief they watched too much television and ate too many takeaways. Wainwright complained that they never went out and that life together in the little flat was getting rather dull. Babcock cried and Wainwright apologised. After she went to bed, he texted his ex-girlfriend.

They were not the only people in the lab who were affected by the death of the mouse. A week afterwards, the lecturer shouted at the cleaner, who promptly dumped him. The lab technician made up with his wife, and the other lecturer could be heard weeping in the loos every morning. None of the students were on speaking terms. The lab was silent, the atmosphere was oppressive. Wainwright and Babcock tried to avoid it as much as possible and tended to spend more time in the library, working on their models of mouse behaviour.

As a result of this work they were invited to give a presentation at a large conference. The last slide in this presentation was a photo of the mouse. It wasn't a great photo, the mouse's fur was ever so slightly blurred, but its face was still charming, its eyes were bright and interested, and its whiskers were fanned out in an inquisitive way. In the lecture theatre, over five hundred behavioural psychologists all looked at this photo and then gazed at one another.

But the mouse's impact was weaker than it had been in the flesh, and the next morning many of the psychologists woke up in the wrong beds, feeling ashamed and confused. There was little discussion at the conference that day. Some people left early, and several promising collaborations that could have led to interesting science never got off the ground.

After Babcock and Wainwright returned home from the conference, they went to the pub to have a serious talk about their relationship. Wainwright said he was feeling tied down, and Babcock had to remind him that he'd been the one who wanted to move in together.

There was another problem; the paper was ready to submit to a scientific journal, but they couldn't agree on which of them should be the first author.

'It should be Wainwright and Babcock,' said Wainwright.

'Nonsense. It must be Babcock and Wainwright,' said Babcock.

They had done exactly equal amounts of work on this paper, and everything was beginning to seem rather unfair to them. So the paper had to wait while they argued.

Wainwright went out drinking more often and came home smelling of beer and perfume. The lab technician resigned, and one of the lecturers went on long-term sick leave. Two students failed their PhD vivas.

Maybe, Babcock thought, things would get better if they found another mouse to love. It seemed very unlikely; they'd worked with many hundreds of lab mice before encountering this one. And because the other mice had disliked it, it could never have mated, and so there were no offspring to carry its genes.

But it couldn't have been the only lab mouse ever to be so appealing to humans. Babcock scoured the scientific literature on mice to see if anything similar had ever happened previously and found a few possibilities. One paper had a footnote to say that the mouse under study was 'delightful' and had been named Daisy. Another paper acknowledged the research councils, the head of the lab and 'a lovely white mouse who helped us with our experiments'. Another had a postscript which said that the two authors got married shortly after submitting the paper. She showed this to Wainwright, who glared at her.

'We could become Babcock and Babcock,' she said. 'That would solve the problem with the paper.' It was supposed to be a joke, but Wainwright wasn't in the mood, and they had the same argument all over again.

The lab was a sad place now. There was an emptiness to it even though it was full of cages of mice and sacks of their feed and straw, and the shelves were cluttered with manuals and notebooks. Babcock couldn't stand it anymore. She couldn't bear to look at the other mice; they repelled her.

Very early one morning, she went into the lab without turning on the overhead lights, to avoid waking the sleeping mice. She tiptoed over to the row of cages and flipped open all the doors. Then she tiptoed out. She spent the day at home, and while Wainwright was working, she packed his belongings into boxes and stacked them in neat piles by the door so that he would find it easier to take them away.

When he returned, he told her about the escaped mice running everywhere in the lab and causing chaos, before he noticed his belongings. Then he wondered out loud who had set the mice free and ruined all the experiments. Babcock didn't bother to reply.

After he'd left, she thought that she might have had enough of mice for the time being. Then she went online to look for a cat to adopt. There were several photos of suitable cats and they all looked so appealing. She was finding it quite difficult to choose, until she found one which was advertised as being a good mouse catcher.

Distant relatives of the Samsa family

When you agree to meet the woman for a coffee in the least fashionable district of Lwów on the first fine spring day of 1940 and, when you choose a table hidden in the dim recesses of the café, you observe her discreetly scratching the upper regions of her legs, you might conclude that she has a skin condition. But you will (equally discreetly) ignore the small, slightly desperate circles of her fingertips as they ceaselessly move back and forth because you are so keen to find out just why she has asked to see you.

As you drink your coffee you note that it is not in fact real, each sip of the chicory-flavoured liquid tells a larger story, each ersatz mouthful is a synecdoche for food shortages and rationing, and worse. And if the woman is still scratching, then perhaps the problem lies with her stockings. New stockings, if they're available at all, are manufactured from a sort of rayon fibre which shines well. Too well, too consistently. Rayon is an indoor lightbulb compared to the natural sunlight of silk.

After the very small coffees have been drunk to the last bitter drop, the woman says that she's enjoyed seeing you again but that she has to go to a meeting, 'No, it's not a doctor's appointment.' But even as she says this, she's still pressing the tips of her fingers against her skirt as if trying to quench a physical urge. And from this you deduce that she's not telling you the truth and that she does indeed have an assignation with a medical professional. A lying woman, you conclude as you summon the waiter, has a desire to tell stories. A lying woman is an interesting woman. You ask if she wants to meet again. She nods. 'Yes, of course,' she says, she has not even begun to explain what happened.

'"When Galia Schmule awakes one morning after a night of uneasy dreams she discovers herself altered in her bed…"'

The woman is reading this to you from a small and battered notebook. You're in the café again, a week after you first met her here. You glance at the pages of her open notebook, the handwriting as cramped as mathematical equations squeezed onto each short line.

'"…into some sort of unclean animal not suitable for sacrifice."' And she closes the notebook and presses her hands against her skirt in a way you are rapidly becoming accustomed to. You know the original story, of course, and you know it doesn't belong to this woman. But why has she changed it? Is the story itself going to be subjected to a metamorphosis, just as the original character is?

And as she says the word 'sacrifice,' the woman's eyes become unfocused, as if she might be seeing something else, and not what is right in front of her. Not the café with its worn velvet banquettes, and waiters wrapped in their long aprons, and newspapers hanging from wooden poles, and Soviet soldiers lounging at the best pavement tables soaking up the sunshine. (You hope the soldiers don't bother to venture this far inside the café.) Let her be imagining another scene entirely, something better than this city that is forced to change its name, like an animal adopting a new camouflage, each time it is occupied or invaded.

When Galia Schmule awakes one morning after a night of uneasy dreams, she finds herself altered. Her bed in the corner of her childhood bedroom looks the same, the bedspread with its cheerful printed fabric of apples and cherries is tucked around her, she can reach out and touch the nearby stove, still warm from its overnight fuel, the tiles smooth beneath her hands, the sunlight is in the right place on the rug, but everything has – overnight – utterly changed. She looks at her hands outstretched on the bedspread, small pale fingers that cannot span an octave on the piano downstairs. The hands are naked, but soon she will be wearing a metal ring on one of them, like a ring through the nose of a farmyard animal –

'Good morning, sleepyhead!' her mother's voice is louder and clearer than usual, as if she is speaking for the benefit of an invisible audience. Galia shrinks down under the covers, trying not to look at her mother's face, not wanting to see how happy and proud she appears. 'Time for breakfast! You've got an important appointment, remember?'

She cannot avoid her fate. She swings her legs out of the bed and walks to the window with its view over the street that the older neighbours still refer to as Krakauer Straße, the morning view of delivery boys bent double under the weight of parcels, and children accompanied by mothers or maids on their way to the school that she once attended. 'I don't feel well, Mama,' she whispers to the window, 'I think I should stay inside today. Not go out anywhere.'

When she was still at school, her mother was only too keen to make her take time off; at least two days each month she was required to lie flat on a sofa with her feet as high as her head. But now – 'Nonsense,' says her mother, 'your monthlies were last week! Don't you want to look at fabric for your wedding dress?'

She leans her forehead against the kind, cool glass. *No.* No, she doesn't. She's become the main character in a story she has read so many times that she knows the plot off by heart. Now she turns around and faces her mother. 'A sacrificial lamb, that's me.' She knows this is wrong, this isn't what the character should be saying. And because it isn't in the story, her mother can't hear her.

'They're all waiting downstairs. They're so proud of you!'

And so she gives up, and lets herself be carried along by the general air of excitement.

This time the coffee is real. You don't know where they managed to get it from, because coffee beans are precious currency in this city. Perhaps the Soviet soldiers are responsible. And the woman is there before you, her notebook lying on the small table. 'I've already ordered for you,' she says as you ease yourself onto the bentwood chair, and sniff the scent of the coffee. At the back of the café is the delightful whirr of beans being ground. Maybe things in Lemberg-Lemberik-Lviv-Lwów will be better from now on.

'I only have forty-five minutes today,' and before you can reply, she slowly raises the hem of her skirt, revealing bare legs up to her knees and then a bizarre arrangement of flat little boxes strapped to her thighs.

'What on earth – '

'I'm an experiment,' she explains, but of course it's no explanation at all. You've seen other Jewish people wear similar boxes like this on their bodies, strapped tightly to their foreheads and left arms. But those were pious men and their boxes contained holy texts from the Torah. What do the woman's boxes contain? As the waiter approaches, she lets her skirt fall so that the boxes are once more hidden, and she opens her notebook and reads to you.

Galia doesn't fit the wedding dress, no matter how many times they alter it. They take it in, and they buckle her into a corset so tight she can barely breathe, before they take pity on her and release her. They try the opposite approach, unpicking the seams and letting the dress out, but then it simply slithers down the length of her body, leaving her standing shivering in her undergarments.

The dressmaker sighs and shakes her head, 'I've never seen anything like this. I took her measurements so carefully, too! I don't know what's wrong!' The woman's on the verge of tears, and so is Galia's mother, silent, pale. The wedding is in six weeks and Galia has nothing to wear.

She gazes at the three of them in the full-length mirror, the woman crouched on the floor with pins sticking out of her mouth, her mother staring fixedly at the silk fabric, so brilliantly white that a single pinprick of blood would destroy it. The dress with its floor-length skirt, full sleeves and embroidery around the neckline doesn't match her narrow dark face, which looks blurred and out of focus in its mirror reflection. Her hands resting against the fabric look like they've been superimposed from another reality that she needs to figure out how to reach. The problem is that the dress belongs in the story, and she doesn't. She's writing herself out of it, she just hasn't decided how.

The dressmaker is arguing with Galia's mother. 'You've already had five sessions,' she says, 'that's more than usual. I can't keep giving you more time. I can't afford it. I've got my other clients, too, you know.'

Galia knows her mother can't afford it either. It would be different if her father were still alive. The story of what happened when he came home from the fighting in 1919 has been told to her and her sisters so many times; how her mother wouldn't let him into the house until his uniform had been removed and abandoned outside, its seams all blackened and charred where they'd been burnt by a lit match to kill the lice and how it hadn't worked because he'd still become ill with typhus. How he lay sweating and fevered in bed, muttering about other soldiers like him returning home from the battlefields, the trains crammed full of suffering men, the corpses flung out of railway carriages as they journeyed east. Delirious, her mother said, but Galia guessed he'd been telling the truth.

Nevertheless her father recovered from that disease, only to succumb to tuberculosis a few years later. Galia is too young to remember the details but she has a single image in her mind of the house after the death, the family sitting shiva on low stools and how she'd thought everyone else was crouching down on these child-sized chairs because they wanted to play with her.

To a louse a human must be as vast as a farm, a district, a collective, an entire oblast, she thinks. A pinprick of blood, that's all it would take.

And her husband-to-be? He's a lad as nervous as herself, and as unwilling, she'll bet. The two of them both sacrificed to an idea of respectability because 'only lower-class people marry for love,' her mother said, and to be respectable was so important in this city where Jews had little else to protect them.

She'd first met him at the Seder earlier that year, covertly watching him as he sat between his parents and tried not to yawn with boredom while her uncle read from the Haggadah, told the tale of the Israelite tribes that had been enslaved and were now free. Except she would never be free. She'd helped her mother prepare the Seder plate, arranging on it the bundles of herbs, the egg, the bowl of salt water, the horseradish, and now she thought of how much these foods represented bitterness, sadness and tears.

Earlier that day, her mother had asked her to collect the lamb bone from the kosher butchers and bring it home to cook. The butcher was on the square which was now called Staryi Rynok and which had been called Ringstraße until the end of the Austrian Empire. Each place in the city had a before and after name, and even though the empire had ended over twenty years ago, and after that there had been the short-lived Republic of the Western Ukraine before this city fell yet again to the Poles, the old names could still be seen in faint ghostlike letters on the stone walls. After the wedding, she would also have a different name and she would only be able to remove the gold ring and whisper her before name when nobody else could see or hear her.

She disliked intensely the task of cooking the lamb bone because it had to be roasted, which meant she had to stand next to the oven, holding it over an open flame, turning it around and around until the flesh darkened and firmed. The fat dripped onto the flame, causing it to flare, and the whole dreadful mess had the sweet smell of death. Although some meat remained on the bone, nobody was allowed to eat it, so it sat on the Seder plate the entire evening – a reminder of all the sacrifices once made long ago. Afterwards she scrubbed her hands with the soap used for cleaning floors, but she could still smell the dead lamb on her fingers as if she'd slit its neck herself.

Now, in front of the dressmaker's mirror, she hears her mother sigh and whisper 'You're doing it on purpose.' But she's doing nothing. She's not required to do anything, that's not her function, other than stretch out on the marital bed as cold as the butcher's slab, and submit.

Only clean and kosher animals can become sacrificial, unclean ones are not deemed worthy. As she lets the chilly white silk fall to the floor she realises, that's the way to avoid my fate – by becoming unclean.

I could do it through sex, she thinks. Lose my virginity, maybe even get pregnant.

No. There must be another way.

She returns home and gets into bed.

In the café, you lean forward. 'Lice?' you say. She nods. Yes, lice.

While she is lying in bed, she looks at her old schoolbooks. Flipping the pages of a biology textbook, she reads about the life cycles of the tapeworm, the flea, the louse – parasites that need human hosts. She stays in bed all day, reading. Her mother enters the room, exasperated. The wedding's in less than a month and there's so much to do.

She agrees, there is a lot to do. But she won't get out of bed so the doctor is summoned, who announces that there is nothing physically wrong with her, so another sort of doctor, a psychoanalyst, comes to the house. She's made aware that this is costing her mother too much money, money that should be more usefully spent on her dowry.

When the psychoanalyst arrives, she doesn't want to see him, but he's used to this sort of behaviour so he fetches a dining chair and sits outside her room, talking through the keyhole. He tells her to open up about her true feelings for her father, and she replies with the story about the lice-infested uniform being burnt in the garden where she used to play. The psychoanalyst diagnoses a fear of growing up, of becoming a proper woman. She's obviously anxious about blood, about menstruation and about childbirth. It's clear she's trying to avoid her fate.

Galia is not afraid of blood, and she has worked it all out. After a week spent in bed, she gets up one morning and eats a decent breakfast. 'At last,' says her mother. 'Good. Here's the shopping list. I want you to go to Feinbergs and order the canapés. Make sure you get the chicken liver pâté. And you must get your hair done, it looks shocking.'

She nods, and leaves the house. But she does not go to Feinbergs and order canapés, nor does she go to the hair-dresser's. Instead she walks right across town to a large, square building near the university. A building she has walked past all her life, but today she enters through the glass doors and approaches the reception, where she asks the questions she has rehearsed many times while at home in bed. An hour or so later, she returns home and tells her mother that she has found a solution to the problem of the wedding dress.

She has rehearsed this as well, and predicted her mother's response.

'Disgusting!' her mother will cry, 'Unclean! How could you, particularly after your father – '

Galia will wait, silent, while her mother's voice rises, 'No man will touch you now! Your fiancé won't want to marry you! You'll never be a mother!'

Good, thinks Galia.

'And your siblings? What about them?' Here her mother's voice will become quieter.

'What about my siblings?' Each of her younger sisters has a new dress which fits them better than her wedding dress fits her. They can still use the dresses, even if the wedding doesn't go ahead.

Here, Galia fails to predict what will in fact happen, that far from remaining hysterical and teary, her mother will take her by the hand and lead, no – *drag* her so that Galia stumbles on a rug and almost falls, and still with her hand gripped in her mother's, she is led into a bedroom and her mother shuts the door, very quietly.

'Galia,' her mother says, 'sit.' And Galia sits upon the bed that used to be her parents' until her father died in here.

Three weeks, she thinks, it will take me three weeks to feed a colony of lice.

Her mother opens a large square book and props it on the satin counterpane. 'Look,' her mother says, indicating the rows and columns of numbers. The household accounts. 'This is what I do each night, after you and your sisters are in bed, I try and make these numbers balance so that the outgoings match up with the income. But it can't be done. We have almost nothing left, Galia. We're living off the jewellery that your dear father bought me when we got married.'

Galia thinks, in three weeks I will have fed eight hundred lice who will then be injected with the typhus bacterium. What an achievement for an eighteen-year-old.

'What about the dowry?'

'What about it? Your uncle is providing it.'

Oh.

And she thinks, everything is numbers. Dowries, dresses, pins, lice, canapés, the world is both tied together and undone by numbers.

'I had hoped – ' her mother starts to say, 'I had hoped that you would understand. How things are. Where we are. What I need you to do.'

Once Galia thought that when a man and a woman got married, there was some semblance of symbiosis between them, that they relied upon each other. That they propped each other up. Her father certainly needed her mother to nurse him in his last illness. But this, as the columns of dwindling numbers in this book reveal, is not true. What is being required of her is more of a parasitism. She is being graphed onto another family tree, like those balls of mistletoe one sees hanging off oak trees. Or even, she shudders, like the fungi on wood. Jew's ears.

'Do *they* know?' Galia asks.

'Who? Of course they do. That's how it works.' But now her mother shuts the book and doesn't look at Galia as she motions at her to get up off the bed, so the satin counterpane can be smoothed flat and there will be no evidence of this conversation.

Of course not, thinks Galia. The pale lad who doesn't want to get married to her, but nevertheless has been told that it's an excellent opportunity for his family. What effort has gone into pretending that their families are equal! That they balance. The large and expensive Seder dinner was probably also funded by her uncle. Whereas Galia and her mother and sisters will in fact be a dead weight.

After a few cycles of louse-feeding, and after she has moved out of the family home and is lodging with the family of one of the scientists, she gets in touch with the pale lad. Offers to meet him at his favourite café and explain to him what happened, if he's interested, if he's not too angry with her. And he is interested. All he knows is that the wedding was called off when Galia's family announced that she was suffering from a debilitating illness, even though she could be regularly spotted walking around town. He felt nothing but relief when the wedding was cancelled, even as his parents started to speculate about the next possible bride. To know that Galia is, in fact, not ill is the most intriguing thing about her he has yet discovered. He wants to know more. He will buy her a coffee.

You have explained to me how it works, how the colonies of lice feed upon their human hosts for two weeks, living in their boxes and separated from the humans only by a fine mesh made from the sieves originally used by peasants to sift their wheat. Then the lice are removed and injected with the typhus before being placed on the humans again, for another five days. At the end of this time, the lice are killed and the contents of their stomachs are pulverised and used as a vaccine.

'We host the same lice before and after they are infected,' you tell me.

'Do you feel any difference?' I ask, 'Can you tell they're infected?'

You shake your head. 'You know, I enjoy it. It takes me beyond myself.' You hold out your hands to me as if to prove to me how clean they are. 'When all the volunteers sit in the institute and the nurses strap the boxes to our legs, we all chat together. I've learnt so much, thanks to the lice! Poetry, mathematics, politics...' Your voice is quiet, reminiscent. Intimate. For a moment, I'm jealous.

'And the danger?'

'There really isn't much danger. The new vaccine works. We have all been injected with it and we might get a few fevers, but none of us ever becomes seriously ill.' You look down and read from your notebook: '"As each louse feeder awakes one morning, they find themselves transformed not into a giant insect, but rather a hybrid creature of human and louse, a *Mischling*."' You close the notebook and I realise I'm inspecting your face. Perhaps this is the first time I have properly looked at you.

Now when we drink our coffee, we must be careful which café we choose. We can no longer go to the old one, because it is favoured by the Nazis. This city is changing yet again; this year has brought with it the withdrawal of the Soviets and the arrival of the Germans. Perhaps they will rename it, call it Lemberg yet again, wipe out its recent history. There are people here who would welcome that, even as the posters go up around the city announcing that Jews are nothing more than pests that spread diseases.

'It's not safe for you, Galia, not for any of us,' I say to you. We're sitting in a corner of a café that is near the institute; you are obviously at home here. Surrounding us are other volunteers, I can recognise the signs now. The outlines of the boxes, the stifling of the urge to scratch.

'It's not as unsafe as it might be,' you reply enigmatically, and then you explain the benefits.

That is why, in a few months' time, when an SS officer approaches us in the café and asks to see our papers, we will each show him the agreements we have signed with the institute that explains we are volunteers on the vaccination programme, and he will read this carefully before taking a step back and dismissing us from his attention. Even though we're 'verminous Jews', a metaphor made literal with our insect-filled tefillin, the Nazis need a typhus vaccine as much as the Poles and the Soviets did, and they know the institute is successfully developing one. And we will pat the boxes on our legs and thank the lice for protecting us.

We are utterly reliant on them now, and so we will feed them for as long as they want.

Safety Manoeuvres

In her spare time Eva likes to grow fruit. With the weekend sun hot on her head, she methodically works her way up and down the strawberry plants, squatting on the damp earth to inspect each one, rearranging the protective straw beneath it and checking for hungry insects. But sometimes the rain arrives before she can finish, and she has to retreat to the kitchen, watching the water strike the small garden with an intensity that she can never get used to, no matter how many years it has been since the storms started.

The fruit is taken to work and appreciated by her colleagues. Today, they all help themselves to berries and gather round Eva's screen to inspect the most recent footage, because Ariel has a problem.

Over the previous few months, the rover has been making its way around a segment of Martian terrain, but now it has run into a patch of dust that is softer than predicted, and consequently its wheels are spinning ineffectively and wasting battery power. Eva and the others have three hours to work out what to do and upload the necessary commands to the control centre in Darmstadt, which will then be relayed forward to the satellite orbiting Mars, and from there beamed down to Ariel. If they don't achieve this in the allocated time, a whole day will be wasted and they'll be the ones catching the flak from all the analysts.

Eva wishes the analysts would learn from Ariel. The rover is capable of assessing its own situation, and will run through a pre-programmed series of movements designed to free itself from the most common sorts of hindrances. If this doesn't work it will quietly wait to be told what to do. It will not phone her up and demand that she detonate one of the mini explosives in its wheels, an act of last resort that would severely impact its future ability to move. It will not email her boss and complain about her. It will not draw her attention to the endless requirements to produce good news stories about it to appease its investors.

'OK, folks,' she says, a strawberry stem cupped in her left hand, 'any thoughts?' And she knows her team will – almost as calmly as Ariel itself – work out the most efficient code to get the rover up and running again.

Each evening, Eva makes her own journey from the office to her flat via the gym. Unlike Ariel's exploration of new territory, Eva's is a well-trodden route. Under a London sky permanently greyed by rainclouds and pollution, as if prematurely aged, she imagines distant Ariel enacting the commands she has sent to it as she tries not to slip on the wet and uneven pavements.

Five minutes to go before yoga starts. She hurries into her sweatpants and takes her usual place next to the mirror so she can check her form. Eva balanced on her hands and feet feels like she could stay there for an unknown length of time, gazing down at the mat and knowing that under the thin layer of rubber lies the wooden floor, and beneath that the concrete and steel foundations of this nondescript building forking down into London clay. Clay that's been seeded during thousands of years with broken brick and fragments of bomb casings and human remains and animal bones and glass fragments and pottery shards, and all the other remnants of previous long-gone civilisations.

'It's such a break, isn't it.' After the class another woman in the changing room is easing her hair out of a tight ponytail. 'Helps us forget everything.'

Eva nods politely but doesn't speak. Nothing helps her forget what's happening.

Later, when she's standing on the platform waiting for the Tube, she feels stale air rush out of the tunnel. Everything is exhausted here, already used up and second hand with no promise of anything better. That night the rain is even worse than usual; all she can do is stand and watch from the kitchen as it batters the plants.

The next day brings yet another problem; Ariel appears to be jammed right up against a boulder and unable to move. It shouldn't have got so close but the terrain in this quadrant wasn't pre-surveyed to a high degree of accuracy, which means errors in Ariel's positioning are more likely, and their job is correspondingly made more difficult.

Eva and her boss are summoned to an online meeting with the analysts, who talk about promising features that need to be investigated within the next 48 hours. They want assurances that the rover will be up and running by the end of today. Eva watches the screen version of herself raise her eyebrows, 'Ambitious. First we have to work Ariel free. And then we need to check it for injuries.'

'"Injuries", Eva? Isn't that a bit anthropomorphic?' the chief analyst comments.

But with its twin stereoscopic lens-eyes tilted at a slight but fetching angle on an elegantly long neck above its stocky little body, Ariel has been consciously designed to appeal to policy makers, to taxpayers and most of all to investors. They don't see what is hidden in that body: the twin tools of mass spectrometer and metal probe. Ariel is capable of drilling into the Martian surface to a depth of one metre, far deeper than any previous rover, before crushing and analysing samples of rock. At this depth things become interesting, according to the analysts, the potential is there for some really useful stuff. Stuff that could be profitably dug up on much larger scales.

'I'll see what I can do,' says Eva. The analysts smile and say of course, with a veneer of politeness shallower than Ariel's probe.

Back in her office, she places her bag on the floor. Then she gets into position; downward dog with hands and feet mirroring each other, so that her right foot is just nudged up against the bag, before she bends her left arm. Ariel has always had a slight weakness in its left front wheel, and she knows by now that this is the best way of mimicking it.

Then she waits and considers, because injuries are always more likely when people act hastily.

A colleague appears at her door and stands watching, appreciating. This is what Eva is good at. This is what she's known for, throughout the whole organisation.

Eva looks at her colleague, apparently upside down and framed by legs, and they smile at each other. Only now does Eva move, very slowly and gracefully lifting her right hand and foot simultaneously just above the rough carpet, angling them slightly away from true and setting them down again, about a centimetre in front of their previous positions.

'Has the bag moved, Lenny?'

Lenny shakes her head, 'No, you're clear.'

Eva repeats the manoeuvre and her right foot is now in front of the bag, 'That should do it.'

'All the effort that they're putting into finding analogue locations on Earth to test the future rovers, in Hawaii and Morocco and everywhere else. And here you are, in an office in South London, perfecting it.'

Eva stands up and brushes her hands clean of crumbs and dust. 'Fifteen degrees, Lenny. Let's code it.' And Lenny nods.

The clay that supports London has long been riddled and punctured with cellars and stations and cables and tunnels and mines, so nobody should be surprised that it's now giving way under pressure from the water. That evening Eva's standing outside the gym when there's a loud crack and a wrenching sound, as if someone is levering the ground open against its will, followed by a human scream and a hiss of bus brakes and a car horn (later she's surprised at her ability to remember all these different noises in sequence), before – silence. A sinkhole has burst right in the middle of the bus lane, about twenty metres away.

Fascinated, she approaches it. The tarmac has split around the edge, and the middle is churned rubble and water. About two metres deep, she estimates. She's not used to taking much notice of her immediate surroundings, but now the city must be considered as carefully as the Martian terrain she analyses each day. She stares at the high street as if she's never before seen the hieroglyph numbers and stripes painted on the road. More car horns start up in the distance as she walks off. But what else can she do? London is being hollowed out, washed away.

A few weeks later and Eva's using the treadmill in the gym. She enjoys the feeling of running on this smooth, slightly yielding surface, as well as being in control over all the relevant variables allowing her to predict every aspect of her movement. She's facing a mirror that allows her to watch other people in the room: a man sitting on a low bench by the shelf of free weights, another standing by the pull-up bars.

But something is not quite right. Her left leg aches; perhaps she has pulled a muscle. There's a peculiar constancy to this ache, as if whatever's wrong is not connected to anything else in her body, as if it's completely autonomous. She drops the incline and speed on the treadmill and continues running, looking at the reflected twin-legs. The way that her feet lift and know exactly where to place themselves is slightly mesmerising, reminding Eva of the beginning of the mission when Ariel first landed, and nobody in the team could stop watching it as it moved in response to their commands across this new territory.

Suddenly she slips and comes crashing down, only just managing to hit the emergency stop button before she lands in a heap on the rubber surface. Dazed and winded, she can't move at first. What the hell happened? She scrabbles around, trying to get her hands underneath her body and push herself up. But someone else is grabbing her and hoisting her until she finds herself propped against the front of the treadmill.

'Easy now,' a man is peering into her face, 'You alright?'

She blinks at him and straightens out her left leg. The knee is still hurting, but no more than it did before. Is it responsible for what happened? She's not sure.

'Going too fast, maybe? Trying to run before you can walk?' He's so close she can feel his breath on her hair as he laughs at his own joke. He holds out a hand, 'Come on, let's get you stood up,' and Eva really doesn't have any alternative but to let him.

His name is Tom, and he won't go away. Before she can stop him, he tells her a lot of things about himself. He's a regular at the gym, here every day since he got made redundant. 'Seen you before,' he says, and now she's horrified that he's already noticed her, that she's left some sort of imprint on him like a tyre track on sand.

'What's *your* name?'

'Ariel,' Eva answers without thinking, surprising herself.

A pause, 'Pretty name. Fancy a coffee sometime, Ariel?'

'I'm a robot actually. I'm designed to move around on the surface of Mars.'

He glances at her more closely, trying to work out if she's joking.

'I grind up rocks and blast them with a laser to find out what they're made of. But now I'm broken,' and she touches her left knee.

He's silent, watchful, perhaps a bit fearful. Waiting to see what she'll do next.

'I'm going back to the lab now to be mended. Goodbye, Tom.'

He nods goodbye and backs away, still watching her. When she's outside, she reaches up her hand to the rain-sodden sky as if the rover is within touching distance.

Over the next week the rain gets even heavier, and one evening when she's just about to go to bed, she hears a rushing noise from the bathroom. Opening the door, she expects to find rainwater splashing in from the open window, but is confronted instead by a fountain of water bubbling upwards from the shower drain. What was kept safely beyond the boundary of her flat, no matter how extreme, has now forced its way inside with an energy that will no longer be contained.

She cannot stop looking at the fountain of dark water, even as it's cascading onto the floor, soaking her bathmat and dressing gown, and more water keeps roaring at her, like a Tube train endlessly coming out of a tunnel. She is frozen, watching the water gushing for endless minutes until finally it slows down and gurgles for a bit, and after that there is silence.

She spends the rest of the night mopping up and cleaning. Removing dead leaves and other debris accumulated on the tiles, wringing water from sodden towels. In the morning it sounds like a bathroom again, with a steady quiet plink of a dripping tap and nothing more.

This flood is a 'once in a lifetime event' according to the media. But that phrase is used at least once a month to describe extreme weather events, so perhaps their life-times are shrinking, being washed away. And after all that mopping up, her left knee is hurting even more, but there's still nothing to see when she examines it. Perhaps she's imagining the pain, hasn't spent the night watching the inside of her flat being invaded by the outside world.

As if in compensation for her bad night, Ariel is working well today. It has made two samples of the soil around it and sent back the resulting data, and for once the analysts are happy, 'This is just what we need to get more invest-ment and grow the company.'

But when she returns home, yet another problem man-ifests itself; the middle of her garden has now dipped into an almost circular crater, about three metres across. Strawberry plants are still clinging onto one side, but she is afraid to walk on this inclined earth. Is it due to subsid-ence in the building's foundations? Has the sewage system simply given way?

If this were Mars, she could code Ariel to probe this disturb-ance and measure the density of the soil, before deciding whether it was safe to be traversed. She lowers herself care-fully onto a small patch of level ground and contemplates the crater, peering closer at the epicentre, where something glints amidst the mud. It's a piece of metal pipe, barnacled with rust. A tool, or a weapon?

Neither Eva nor her neighbours are surprised when the police arrive and cordon everything off. 'For your own safety,' they're told. Tests will have to be carried out before they'll be allowed to go into the garden again. No, nobody can say how long this might take, there's a backlog of tests to be done.

Eva stands in her kitchen and looks at the distant garden, framed by the window. She wonders what she can offer her colleagues now that the strawberries are out of bounds.

'Listen, we appreciate your empathy for the little guy,' says one of the analysts, 'you obviously have a knack for knowing how to handle him! How to get the best from him.' Eva can feel Lenny roll her eyes. 'But we need to push forward. It's all about growth. We've got to explore more terrain and do it quicker. You're always very careful and thorough, and that's admirable, but from now on things are going to be a little...looser. After all – ' he doesn't have to continue because Eva knows the past and future as well as he does. After all, this is not the first Mars rover and won't be the last. Ariel is merely the latest in a series of increasingly ambitious commercial expeditions. 'Space oil' has been promised to investors, the chance to turn the alien rocks of Mars into profit.

So the analysts want Ariel to move to a new quadrant, one which might have a higher density of metal ores. Eva and her boss study maps to try to work out the best route for Ariel, but the ground is littered with rocky debris, and when they zoom in on the relevant images, they see some worryingly sharp edges that could damage the rover's wheels.

'Tricky,' says Eva.

Her boss shrugs, 'Just give them what they want.'

She returns to her office and calculates a route that will require the fewest manoeuvres and expose Ariel to the least potential for damage. She envies the rover its opportunity to make a wholly new journey that has never been made before, across terrain that has never been subjected to footfall. She considers her daily commute, nothing more than a scribble back and forth on a planet that's all used up.

Is this why she gives Ariel a slightly longer route than necessary to reach the latest zone of interest, to allow it a chance simply to experience this new world without having to work? When it's not drilling, the analysts aren't scrutinising it. It can simply be. She inserts into the code a pause to Ariel's route, where it will do nothing for a whole Mars hour.

A chance for it to fully recharge its batteries in sunlight, she argues at the next meeting. The rest of her team look at her. They know this isn't necessary but they don't say anything in front of the analysts.

Ariel has four years left, and after that its battery will fail. Although they will still be able to view it from the small comms satellite that orbits Mars, it will sit motionless, uncommunicative, silent. It will join the ranks of other defunct rovers that nobody bothers about anymore, marooned here and there like sentries guarding treasures they cannot comprehend.

After Ariel reaches the new quadrant, it's programmed to drill a rapid series of holes in a grid-like formation. Each hole yields about a kilogram of ground-up rock which Ariel deposits in its mass spectrometer, carries out a chemical analysis and transmits the results back to the team. A mutation of matter into numbers. All this keeps Eva busy for several weeks.

When she first started work here, nobody told her the rover had a voice. Ariel is silent when they all watch it on the screen, it only speaks to her when she's by herself, writing the code for the next day's movements. Then it speaks as the ancient oracle at Delphi might have done, in formless streams of bytes that spool out of it, a deluge of numbers that surge up as if from the depths of that distant planet on which it crawls. And sometimes Eva sits quiet and still and gazes at this gift: pure numbers not yet sullied by their transformation into 'investment opportunity' or 'mining potential'.

During this time, the river bursts its banks further downstream of Eva's flat. What was once land is now submerged, boundaries are under water, borders are washed away. Part of the Tube network has been knocked out and some bus routes are diverted, others are cauterised into shorter sections. Eva works from home every day now, only going outside in rubber boots to wade up the road and buy food. She misses being with the team and the way they nibbled at her strawberries, making each precious fruit last.

On Mars, Ariel's drill bit shatters. It's able to deploy a backup, but 'It's been working too much,' Eva tells the analysts, 'it needs a break.'

The analysts sigh.

'Why don't you make a story out of this? Something interesting for your investors?' She knows they can't read her, can't tell if she's being sarcastic or not.

'You know what the story is, Eva. It's the one where time is money and we've got to beat the competition.'

'It's a game and we've got to take risks to get to the next level.'

Everything they say has to be decoded to get at the hidden damage, she realises. Their words are the surface hiding the deep-down truth that is too dangerous to be exposed to the light.

After the water from the latest flood has been pumped away, the pavements are left slick with debris. Eva, rushing in her rubber boots to the shops, slips and bangs the troublesome left knee, too hard to ignore this time. The ambulance arrives surprisingly quickly; she suspects they simply cruise the city streets looking for casualties of the weather.

Many hours later and she's back in her living room, lying on the sofa. She requests an emergency meeting, 'It's the left leg, I'm afraid. Serious damage.'

The analysts are bleating something about delays, so she interrupts. 'Not sure what caused it. Yes, you can see it in the images.' She was allowed to take the X-rays with her and now she flips through them, admiring the grey moon-like knee and its newly acquired imperfection. A crack on the outside of the patella, she was told. Not a surprise, she thinks, surfaces are giving way everywhere.

Can it be fixed? they're shouting before they gradually fall silent, waiting for her to speak. They don't have the imagination to guess that she's referring to something more organic than a buckled metal strut, that the problem is closer to home.

But Eva doesn't bother to reply. She shelters the phone in her hand, giving it the same attention that she shows to all machines in her care, no matter where they are.

Schrödinger's wife

According to quantum physics, light is said to have a wave/particle duality; depending on how it is being observed at a specific moment in time, it will exhibit one or the other attribute but not both simultaneously. Either the wave-identity of light will propagate here and there through empty space to generate a coherent image of stripes, or the particle-identity of light will strike a metal plate and liberate an electron via an intimate transaction of energy that does not form a visible pattern. This duality might appear contradictory to us, but that is only because of our limited perceptions. Light is an entity that changes its observable characteristics depending on circumstances; its nature is essentially performative.

Furthermore, it's an inescapable aspect of quantum reality that the observer interacts with the experiment to affect the outcome; indeed, the phenomena don't really exist without the observer, so perhaps it is better to talk of these interactions rather than the entities behind them. Yes, that is where we should focus our attention – on the interactions, or relationships.

In December 1925, the physicist Erwin Schrödinger abandons his wife Anny for a few weeks while he goes on holiday to a hotel/sanatorium in the small town of Arosa in the Swiss Alps. Whilst there, he makes a breakthrough discovery about the atom that explains important aspects of its behaviour. During this holiday Schrödinger is allegedly accompanied by a woman whose identity has never been known, and who is often referred to as the 'mystery lover' (according to the standard biography of him by Walter Moore).

Three years prior to the 'mystery woman' episode, in 1922 Schrödinger and Anny journeyed together to the same hotel/sanatorium in Arosa, where he recuperated from a bout of tuberculosis. There she took care of him, ensuring that he spent hours resting outside in the frigid mountain air, and that he had access to jars of oxygen when he needed help to breathe.

Anny and Schrödinger's visit to Arosa is separated by fifteen years and only a few kilometres from the Berghof sanatorium in Davos, which Hans Castorp visits, as described in *The Magic Mountain* by Thomas Mann. In Hans's time, the primary way of diagnosing the illness is by auscultation, a process in which the physician taps the patient and listens to the resulting sounds, diseased cavities in the lungs and other organs producing a pronounced 'hollowness'.

Auscultation was a careful and precise technique, taking physicians years to learn and perform with confidence, but by the early twentieth century it was in the process of being rendered obsolete. As Hans makes the journey to Switzerland, his train passes through the southern German town of Würzburg, where, a few years previously, Wilhelm Röntgen has discovered X-rays in the small laboratory set up in the basement of his family home. In

1922, sanatoria in Arosa and elsewhere that catered for patients with tuberculosis were reliant on X-rays for their diagnoses. When a patient has their X-ray taken, they are required to stay still and silent; the physician has no need to listen either to the sounds made by the patient's body or to the patient discussing their symptoms in an invariably subjective and partial manner. The diagnostic process has become more scientific, more objective.

The 'mystery woman/abandoned wife' dichotomy is as ubiquitous as wave/particle duality in discussions of Schrödinger and his work. But there is nothing in the historical record to contradict the possibility that in 1925 Anny Schrödinger is not 'abandoned' by her husband; rather she simply declines to go on holiday with him, preferring instead to stay at home by herself.

It's 15th December 1925, and Anny and Erwin are standing on either side of an open suitcase in their apartment in Zurich. Erwin is due to catch a train later that day, and he still can't understand why Anny won't be accompanying him.

'I just don't want to go there.' This isn't the first time she has told him this, but it may be the first time he's actually heard her.

He pauses, a notebook in each hand, 'Why on earth not?'

Her desire for time and space by herself will not survive the transformation into words but there might be other reasons that are easier to articulate. 'I've already bought a ticket for a concert at the Tonhalle next week. Brahms. A piano recital.'

He frowns. Pianos are troublesome, they do not talk of pianos and, as Anny predicts, he says no more.

'In any case, the question shouldn't be why I *don't* want to go there, but rather, why you *do* want to go there.' She bends down and stuffs a pair of his hiking socks into the case, releasing a smell as sharp as pine needles but more artificial, more modern. She recognises it from Arosa, it has persisted in the leather innards of the case since they were last there. It is the smell of disinfectant, an essential aspect of the sanatorium's medical regime.

As she recoils from this medical spectre, Erwin sorts through his notebooks, 'It's a peaceful place to work, and I can relax by skiing.' But he doesn't even attempt to make this sound credible.

'A place where you once spent months coughing your guts up doesn't sound particularly peaceful to me.' In any case Anny can guess why he's returning to Arosa, 'She can't still be there, you know. Not after all this time.' (Perhaps Anny has either forgotten, or is not aware of Hans Castorp's lengthy seven-year stay in the Berghof sanatorium…)

'Who?'

Anny doesn't reply. She and Erwin both know who.

Schrödinger is going to Arosa to think about why atoms have been observed to emit and absorb light only at certain allowed wavelengths, and not at other forbidden ones. According to the special theory of relativity, light does not experience time; it exists in an eternal present with neither anticipation of the future nor memory of the past. In contrast, atoms journey through time. Radioactive atoms shed X-rays as they transform themselves and mutate into daughter atoms that bear no trace of their elemental origins.

Perhaps, then, this story is also the story of daughters. Of the girl in Arosa in 1922 who went there to take care of her sick father. Of Max Planck's twins.

Schrödinger was a reluctant revolutionary, a physicist who believed that the world was unaffected by his observing it. He shared this viewpoint with his colleague Max Planck, whose attempt, appropriately on the cusp of the new century in 1900, to calculate the amount of energy emitted by a domestic lightbulb inadvertently started the entire quantum movement. With their rounded fruit-like shape (the German name for them, *Glühbirne*, translates literally as 'glow pear'), lightbulbs bear a familial resemblance to the Crookes tubes used by physicists to produce X-rays in laboratories and sanatoria. And as with Schrödinger, Max Planck is no stranger to sanatoria; in 1909 his first wife Marie dies of tuberculosis. Shortly afterwards he marries Marga, who is Marie's niece and just seven years older than his twin daughters.

Planck can only find an accurate equation that predicts the observed emission of energy from a lightbulb when he suggests ('in desperation', he freely admits afterwards) that this energy must be emitted and absorbed not as a continuum but rather in finite little packets that he calls 'quanta', for which the frequency of the light is v and its associated energy is E. Planck's innovation is to link these two hitherto separate properties of light using a new physical constant h via the relation $E = hv$. (For example, red light has a lower frequency than blue and therefore less energy.) He assumes – perhaps even hopes – that this is just a mathematical trick that bears no relationship to reality, and that future work will render unnecessary this apparently ad hoc 'quantum' aspect of his equation.

More than one hundred years later, no such work has been forthcoming. We are stuck with the quantum.

Pianos are troublesome in the Schrödinger household because Erwin 'does not allow Anny to play' (according to his biography). Nevertheless, there is a mute and shut-up box of a piano in the corner of the parlour, a coffin containing Anny's desire to enjoy herself. He may have forbidden her to play it but he does not own it; the piano belongs to Anny, and she is determined to keep hold of it, its very uselessness a metaphor for what persistently goes wrong between them.

So let us imagine her seated at a quite different and vast grand piano, in a ballroom, say, playing something from her Viennese childhood. A Strauss waltz is the most obvious choice, perhaps "The Blue Danube." Her fingers striking each of the keys with a precision and a timing that her husband will never appreciate, the keys connecting to the hammers hidden within the wooden casing, the hammers hitting the strings, and the strings vibrating and releasing energy at certain, allowed, frequencies.

Where is there a grand piano in a Zurich ballroom that Anny might play? Don't ask Anny, she doesn't know, she hasn't lived here long enough to find out. They must keep moving from city to city so that Schrödinger can pull himself up each rung of the academic ladder. Since their marriage five years ago, they have lived in Vienna, Jena, Stuttgart and Breslau, in addition to that six-month stay in Arosa. She would like not to have to move house again, to have the opportunity to stay still and sit in peace at her piano. Maybe even to sing as well, but that too has been 'discouraged' by Erwin.

By 1925 he is no longer in love with her, indeed perhaps he never was, and only married her on the rebound from another girl, another failed relationship (again, according to the biography). He views Anny as neither intellectual nor attractive – his two main classifications of women; nevertheless, she is there. When he was ill in 1922 she took care of him. He cannot deny that.

But in 1925, as he hurries to the station to catch the train, he does his best to avoid thinking about her alone in their apartment. He doesn't understand her reasons for wanting to remain in Zurich by herself, a city she's never pretended to feel at home in. Furthermore, it will look very odd if he arrives at Arosa without her; a middle-aged man fetching up at a hotel for the Christmas holidays without his wife. Odd, as well as annoying and expensive, because he will still have to pay for her room and board there.

Max Planck's daughters Emma and Grete are identical twins and consequently at school they are in the habit of misleading their teachers; 'I'm not Grete, she is,' insists Grete to a baffled science teacher. They have been asked by the school to wear red (Emma) and blue (Grete) hair ribbons so they can be distinguished from each other, but during the mid-morning break, when they are supposed to be eating their buttered pretzels, they frequently swap these ribbons. Max Planck wonders if this aberrant behaviour is due to their mother's long and distressing illness.

Support for Planck's 'little packet' theory came from Einstein's explanation of the so-called photoelectric effect in 1905 (for which he was awarded the Nobel Prize). This phenomenon occurs when light striking a metal plate liberates electrons from within that plate; a greater intensity of light does not mean that the electrons have more energy, only that more of them are liberated. In Einstein's revolutionary reasoning, this meant that light should be thought of as particles, each light-particle (or 'photon') responsible for liberating each electron. When proposing this, Einstein overturned centuries of thinking that light was a wave, as apparently proved by various experiments showing its ability to be diffracted and refracted.

Nobody (and certainly not her husband) has ever observed Anny with the same degree of scrutiny with which she has repeatedly eyed herself in the mirror and thought, 'unruly hair, thin lips, big nose, sparse eyelashes'. Nobody has judged her as precisely as Anny judges herself, considers the way her knuckles stand proud from her hands like those of a fishwife, the square and blunt ends to her fingers as if her body has come to an abrupt halt.

When she was younger, Anny's mother made her a party dress that gave an illusion of fluttering movement. Brushed her daughter's hair and curled the ends with a hot iron, before smacking her daughter's face to make her seem as if she were blushing becomingly, and sending her into the salon where the other young people were gathered.

Light emitted from a single bulb may be sent through two narrow parallel slits before it spreads out in space and creates a pattern of stripes, a classical demonstration of wave-like properties that was first demonstrated in 1803 by the polymath Thomas Young (he also helped decipher the Rosetta Stone). A straightforward experiment that nevertheless is a mystery, for it is only natural to ask which slit the light travelled through. But by investigating it you destroy the pattern; it exists in the indeterminacy of light's nature, the lack of our knowledge of its path through space and time. A too detailed, too precise observation will affect the outcome of the experiment. Knowing this, Anny's mother advises her daughter to act mysteriously when being introduced to a young man: 'Speak as if you have a long-hidden secret inside you that you aren't at liberty to divulge, for if they know everything about you all at once, they will quickly lose interest.'

But the young men don't appear to spot anything mysteriously interesting about Anny, or think to ask her views on the double slit experiment. Indeed, they scarcely seem to notice her at all, and she becomes accustomed to making lingering visits to the powder room so that she's not such an obvious wallflower. There, she whiles away time by listening to the muffled waltzes and watching herself in the mirror. *I see me.* But is *me* the same entity as *I*? Or has the act of seeing myself in the mirror somehow split me into two? She tries and fails many times to answer this conundrum. *Am I a coherent entity?* As soon as she asks this, she divides herself. The question sets up its own paradox.

Anny will never know Emma or Grete but will in the future (when she moves to Berlin) meet their daughters, born a year apart. Daughters who are not quite sisters but more than cousins; nobody will ever find the exact word to describe their relationship.

Right now in Zurich, with her husband away, Anny is alone. She doesn't cook his dinner, or listen to his complaints about his dull students, or iron his shirt, or sit around waiting for him to come home late in order to reheat that congealed dinner. And she's not required to witness him smiling to himself and rearranging his hair when he does, finally, return. Once there were visible grass stains on the knees of his trousers, 'A last-minute picnic with my colleagues, Anny. You wouldn't have enjoyed it.' More than once, a lilac envelope has tumbled out of his jacket pocket and been hastily consigned to the kitchen range.

Now she dispatches him to the disinfectant-wraithed hotel in Arosa, to the jars of oxygen and the brightly polished spittoons. And although she regularly feels repulsed by the parlour, she enters it now and sits on the sofa; at least the surrounding silence is hers alone and not that of two people who live together and yet not together, who orbit each other without ever coming into contact.

Every time she moves house, she has to drag these rooms along with her, haul their Biedermeier certainties to each new location, like installing a stage set for a play that has long ago ceased to attract any audiences. There is a precise spot on the sofa from where her gaze falls on the following: an engraved image of Erwin's grandfather in his army uniform at the time of the Austro-Prussian war, a set of Goethe's collected works bound in gilded leather and a coffee pot hand-painted with pink rose buds. But the coffee pot is chipped, the Goethe is incomplete, the engraving is marked by circles of mould eating the very substance of the paper. This constellation of imperfect objects includes her; she too feels chipped, marked and incomplete.

She abandons the parlour and takes refuge in the linen closet, burying her hands deep in the piles of freshly laundered sheets so that they are no longer visible, and she's able to imagine those hands in another version of reality. Grinding up uranium ore, like Marie Curie, or positioning delicate gold leaf near a radioactive source, like Lise Meitner. Playing the piano, like her earlier self. By rendering her hands invisible, even if for a brief moment, she allows them a secret freedom the rest of her yearns for.

But she cannot stand half-in, half-out of the cupboard forever. She decides to have a bath and by the middle of the afternoon is reading a novel while submerged in sloshing water, although it has been necessary to scent that water with oil to mask the persistent smell of the pine disinfectant which, peculiarly, has only increased in intensity since Erwin left.

On the third day of her freedom another smell makes its presence felt. Although she has not bothered to order any fresh meat from the butcher just for herself, there is a definite odour of blood in the apartment. Sweet, almost sickly. But it is no stronger in the kitchen or larder than in the parlour or bedroom. Over the next few days, it waxes and wanes, intertwining itself around the disinfectant like a braid of hair.

It must be a sensory hallucination; she's heard of such things. She makes a coffee to steady her nerves, takes it into the parlour and sips. But this liquid doesn't taste of coffee, it has a vegetable, medicinal flavour. She sips again;

the flavour is one that can only be obtained from crushing the leaves of mountain herbs and infusing them with hot water, subsequently to be drunk by a patient suffering from tuberculosis in a Swiss sanatorium. She holds the cup in her two hands, stares into the liquid. Although she can see quite clearly that the cup is one of a set of almost translucently thin porcelain given to them as a wedding present and is not a heavy stoneware mug manufactured to withstand being cleaned at high temperatures in order to kill dangerous bacteria, the weight in her hands tells her otherwise. She sets the cup down on the side table and refuses to look at it.

Anny has a hot bath, reads her book and then dozes on the bed. She is determined to grow used to the smells and tastes and sensations that have taken up residence in the apartment. Perhaps they were always there, but she has simply not noticed them before now because she has had to work so hard to accommodate her husband and all his requirements.

Anny dabs her lips with a handkerchief. She is not eating, has no need of a napkin. She dabs her lips again, she cannot stop herself from doing it. Dab dab. This is what patients in Arosa do, when they fear they are haemorrhaging blood from their lungs into their mouths. Dab dab. She remembers the girl in Arosa and her fear of the illness, she remembers holding the girl's hand. Now she watches in the mirror as her hand meets her mouth.

Dab dab.

It seems Anny is not her own woman any more.

She goes to the bedroom to fetch another handkerchief and opens a drawer, only to find a neat array of lilac envelopes addressed to Erwin at his offices in all of those university departments. Surely these letters can't have been here before now? Did Erwin bring them home before he went off to Arosa? Opening the drawer is bad enough, she will not read the letters, she doesn't want the specifics of his infidelities to be spelled out as clearly and unambiguously as a mathematical equation.

Anny and the drawer confront each other while around her the apartment seems to be holding its breath, and all her future selves wait for her to act.

Meanwhile Schrödinger is attempting to construct an equation which will explain just why electrons orbiting in atoms are only permitted certain energy values. According to him, these electrons behave like a standing wave and therefore must have a whole number of wavelengths, analogous to the strings of a piano that are fixed at both ends and can only vibrate at certain wavelengths. But he wants his model to be more than just a mathematical convenience or analogy, for him the electron really *is* a wave and not a particle. In Schrödinger's worldview, an orbiting electron twangs eternally around its atomic nucleus – whether or not we are present to observe it.

Nobody has seen Anny for several days; she may or may not be in the apartment. She might have slammed shut the drawer containing the lilac envelopes and decided to distance herself from this place that is decidedly not a home. She might have opened the window to let in fresh air before placing her nightgown and washbag into a small case and leaving, catching a tram to the centre of the city to spend a few nights in a hotel.

'You are here by yourself, madam?' The man at the front desk will possibly frown at this irregularity.

She feels him assess her, a tired and unattractive woman. Nothing of interest from the crown of her unfashionably large hat to the tips of her scuffed winter boots. When she has completed the registration form, he reads it and frowns again. She lives just a few kilometres away, why is she staying here, and by herself?

She could say something to reassure this man, but she is weary of having to provide calming words, of removing emotional energy from a room. Let this man feel doubtful about her, let him remember her as the woman whose purpose is not at all clear. Let her apparent motivation for staying in this place at this time be memorably uncertain.

Anny's hotel room is just one of countless possibilities, their doors leading on to a corridor so gloomy its boundaries cannot be glimpsed, it is seemingly endless. The only unique aspect of a hotel room is its number, and finally, after pacing up and down the corridor, peering at the doors, Anny locates hers.

This room is nothing like those in Arosa which are designed to be easy to clean each morning while the guests eat their medically prescribed breakfasts. This one is swathed in fabric; heavy velvet curtains, an equally heavy bedspread, a thick rug, and all of it reinforcing the separation with the outside. She collapses onto the bed and eases off her boots. She does not dab her mouth. All she can smell is the abandoned perfume of a previous guest. Neither blood, nor disinfectant.

Anny is enjoying the symmetry to her and Schrödinger's situations, with both of them staying in hotels. But this symmetry is slightly imperfect because he only thinks he knows where she is.

Every book written about Schrödinger notes his charm, his ease with people. Many books comment on his attraction to women, and his appreciation of them. Anny could have remarked that his charm was very ephemeral indeed, with a short half-life of just a few months. After that, a bitter constancy; what endured were the tempers, the intellectual haughtiness, the unjustified certainty that he was the centre of not only his own life, but also of other people's.

As Anny immerses herself in the bath and admires the distorted reflection of her body in the shining taps, she remembers Ilse or Elsi (Anny was never quite sure of her name), a girl about fifteen or sixteen years old who accompanied her sick papa to Arosa, arriving at the same time as the Schrödingers in the autumn of 1922. Each day her father wheezed his way around the hotel's/sanatorium's rose garden with his hand tucked in her arm, and each evening he played cards and lost heavily. When she wasn't with him, Ilse/Elsi could be seen climbing the steep paths away from the hotel and the village, heading into the heart of the old forest that stood above them.

In an ironic development similar to the fate of Hans Castorp, Ilse/Elsi fell ill herself not long after she arrived at the sanatorium and was required to spend her afternoons wrapped in thick blankets on the balcony, taking prescribed 'air baths'. When Anny asked how she was feeling, Ilse/Elsi opened wide her glassy, feverish eyes but did not reply.

The situation is as follows. If x is a ray of light and also a girl, then there are two possibilities for what has happened. The light has gone through the two slits, undisturbed and unbothered, and as a consequence has behaved as a wave and formed its pattern. If Anny doesn't know which slit the light went through, then there is a possibility that the girl is still alive.

In Zurich, Anny wakes up after a good night's sleep and looks out of the window, the same height as the branches of tall trees that line the pavements in this part of town, and beneath them she can glimpse the brightly coloured hats of passers-by: a red beret here, a purple cloche there. The pale morning sky is also visible, broken up by the trees, but when she moves away from the window, the room itself has assumed the slightly dank feel of a basement. The air is heavy with moisture, the light has dimmed. She is not in a basement, she is on the second floor. She shuts her eyes and is aware of stone walls, she opens her eyes and sees striped wallpaper, an ornate mirror, a framed sketch of St Nicholas.

She must leave the room.

In 1922, Anny goes looking for Erwin and finds him on the public veranda, standing rather too near to Ilse/Elsi, who is resting on a day bed. Guests are required to distance themselves from each other for fear of spreading infections, and Anny reminds Erwin of this rule. Erwin argues briefly before disappearing indoors, and Anny sits on a chair at the correct distance from Ilse/Elsi.

As Anny identifies the distant mountain peaks, Ilse/Elsi compares this landscape with her home near Hamburg. So flat, she whispers. So endlessly and monotonously flat, those northern heaths could drive a person mad. But for some reason her sister likes it. That's why she's the one who came here with their papa, and her sister stayed at home. How lucky she is, to have an adventure like this!

'Your sister?' says Anny.

'*Twin* sister,' says Ilse/Elsi with obvious pride, 'her name is –' but she starts to cough and cannot say anything more for some time.

In Zurich, Anny leaves the hotel and strides along the shore of the lake, eats an indifferent lunch in a restaurant that is indifferently served to her because she is a woman by herself, and visits a bookshop. As she walks the city streets, she notes how they repeat themselves every few metres in the most regular fashion; the city is a wave, and its people are the particles propagating through it.

Anny returns to the hotel later in the afternoon when the sky is already dimming and the buildings are turning into black outlines holed by yellow-lit windows. In her room she sits with a book on her lap, intending to continue reading the story, but for now she will rest.

Anny with her eyes shut senses the basement around her, its moisture creeping at her, stroking her skin and accompanied by a distant sound she cannot quite make out. What of it? Someone is always laughing or crying or shouting in a busy city hotel. But this sound resolves itself into a coughing fit.

The word *auscultation* comes from the Latin 'to listen'. Anny listens as closely as if she has placed her ear on Erwin's chest and hears him, a few hundred miles away and in a parallel basement, demonstrating his cough to the Arosa sanatorium's resident doctor.

This may be the real reason for him wanting to return to Arosa.

'We could take an X-ray,' Anny hears the doctor suggest, 'See what's going on inside you.'

And even though he has made the choice to come here, Erwin is now declining, backing away from a more complete knowledge of what is happening inside him, 'It's just a cough. Not much more than a cold.'

'You're an ex-patient whose lungs are scarred by the disease. In this place you'll inevitably be subjected to possible new outbreaks.'

'Are you suggesting it was dangerous for me to come here?'

The doctor shrugs, 'I suppose you had your reasons.'

Erwin takes his leave and climbs the dank stone steps from the basement up to the hotel's public rooms.

Anny opens her eyes and Zurich reappears, the already-familiar swag of curtain protecting her against the city night and its buildings as regular as bones in an X-ray.

Everything overtly to do with the medical treatment of patients in Arosa was hidden away down those steps, so that the rest of the building could get on with the pretence that it was just an ordinary hotel. But that underground room was a kind of limbo, its walls decorated a futile shade of yellow, a skin-thin disguise that fooled no one. When Anny peered closer at the walls, she fancied she could see old blood stains.

How much time did Anny and Erwin spend in that basement as they waited to be shown his X-rays, with the astringent smell of photographic fluids nipping at their noses? Sitting side by side but not holding hands because nobody, not even married couples, could touch each other in public. The basement was the place where the two of them got into the habit of never touching.

In 1922 Ilse/Elsi asks Anny, 'How old were you when you first met Erwin?'

Anny thinks. It was seven, eight, no, nine years ago. The last summer before the war; Erwin in his summer jacket with that unexpected and gaudy lining, and she in her best embroidered frock.

'The same age as I am now,' says Ilse/Elsi.

Anny contemplates the forested mountains where there are said to be wolves. She is sure she can hear them howling at night, and imagines the twin pinpricks of their eyes as they dare to approach Arosa. In the daytime she discreetly searches the no-man's-land beyond the hotel for evidence, but is not quite sure what she should be looking for. Small and bloodied pieces of fur?

'Did you hear me, Anny?'

Anny continues scanning the landscape. She has learnt not to mention the wolves to Erwin, he will only ridicule her.

In Zurich Anny listens to the thump of Erwin's heart as he walks the public rooms of the Arosa hotel. Searching.

Is *this* the reason he went back?

Thump-thump-thump, his heart quickens as he sees a young girl, but, no, it's not her. Never her. Of course she isn't here, he knows this and yet he can't stop himself walking to and fro, passing through the dining room, the card room and along the veranda. Some of the permanent guests think they recognise him. After all, it hasn't been that long since he was last here – but he slips away from them before anything can be said.

However, he can't avoid talking to Mrs Banner, the hotel proprietress.

'By yourself over Christmas, Herr Doktor Schrödinger? Your good lady wife not with you?' she raises an artificially darkened eyebrow.

'Anny's in the family way,' he lies.

'Family! How wonderful!' Mrs Banner's lemon-hued hairdo fairly shakes with emotion. This is a true success for the hotel! A guest who is not only cured but also able to father children.

'Yes, Anny is delighted, of course. As am I. But the doctor has advised her not to travel. And so here I am,' he spreads his hands out wide.

'Here you are,' she mimics his gesture, smiling.

Anny knows that Erwin's betrayals are numerous. She may as well add a fictional pregnancy to the ever-increasing list.

In 1922 Ilse/Elsi is on the veranda, flipping through a pack of playing cards. 'You want to play?' she asks Anny, who shakes her head. She doesn't exactly disapprove of card games, but all those different possibilities arrayed before her always make her feel vertiginous and light-headed. The girl shrugs, lays a row of cards out on the blanket covering her lap, considers them. 'Do you want to know how I ended up here?' She's still staring at the cards.

'You told me. You chose going away over staying at home,' says Anny, 'You chose southern mountains over northern heaths.'

'That was just a story so that you wouldn't feel sorry for me. The truth is, gambling was involved. A quick game of *vingt-et-un*, lasting no more than a few minutes, settled the fates of me and my sister. I won, or lost, depending on how you look at it.'

Silence, while Anny considers this appalling fact. The cards face down on Ilse/Elsi's lap are as identical and anonymous as bank notes.

'We are all subject to unknown forces, Anny,' Ilse/Elsi continues, 'that blow us hither and thither, transport us along railway lines and propel us up mountains and down valleys. The physical force of gravity, tempered by air resistance, decided how the cards should fall. At least I know this.' She wipes her forehead with a handkerchief embroidered with a monogram so curly and ornate that Anny can't decipher it.

Down the hill from the hotel in Arosa lies a graveyard where the headstones are neat and ordered. Erwin likes to walk here when he's feeling well enough, although Anny thinks it's morbid.

'You need to practice wearing widow's weeds,' he says, attempting gallows humour.

'I'm too young for widowhood, and anyway, you survived worse odds in the war, being shot at by Italians.'

'You're never too young for it, Anny, dear,' and he flicks at something on her shoulder that was once there but is no longer, something that has not existed for several years.

Ilse/Elsi wants to talk about her twin, 'The last time I saw her was when I got on the train to come here and she came to the station to see me off. And you know what Einstein has to say about people and trains, and how it's impossible for them to agree on what they're observing, what they're witness to.'

Anny nods.

'I'm the girl in the train with her Papa, and I watch him light his cigarette, and I see the glow of the match simultaneously illuminate the front and back of the carriage. But my sister, who's waving farewell to us from the station platform as the train moves away, sees this expanding circle of light strike the back of the carriage that is rushing to greet it before the front of the carriage that is fleeing from it.'

'And the girl on the train thinks she is going off for a nice summer holiday in the mountains with their Papa. But the girl on the platform knows that their destinies are diverging, and will never converge again. And nobody can agree on what they see.'

The weather is still warm, but already those distant mountains have lines of snow written in their deeper crevices, lines that highlight the complexities of the surface.

'Were you really forced to play cards like that?'

Ilse/Elsi nods. Her eyes are shut, her cheeks are flushed. Anny watches her chest move up and down with the visible effort of breathing.

'I'm sorry,' says Anny and squeezes her hand in sympathy. This placing of one woman's hand on another is too small to be noticed by the other people resting on the veranda, and yet as a result Ilse/Elsi starts to weep. 'I miss my mother so much,' she whispers. 'I miss my sister too. Papa – '

Papa is a wastrel who spends every evening gambling and does not deserve to have his daughter here, Anny knows. Papa should feel guilty that he has indirectly caused her to catch this disease from which he is evidently recovering, appearing fatter by the day while she – ? Nobody knows her fate but they can all guess.

'Do you want to see something?' Ilse/Elsi is still whispering, but the tears are drying in the sun, and with her free hand she reaches under the blanket and brings out a small dark square of glass marked here and there with an indistinct grey pattern. She gestures with it to Anny, who takes it from her.

'Hold it up to the light,' Ilse/Elsi instructs. They are still holding hands, still connected as Anny obediently lifts the glass up to the sky, and there in front of her are the ribs, the lungs, the spine, the viscera, all the shadows that make up a human body. A body projected onto the surface of the sky, with sunlight pouring through it as if it is being resurrected right in front of her.

'This is you?' asks Anny.

Ilse/Elsi nods, 'I'm thinking of sending it to my sister, so she can see what she's missing.'

'You can't do that, it's not her fault.' Anny's still looking at the miraculous light-filled body, 'Don't make her feel guilty.'

'You're right,' Ilse/Elsi sighs.

'Give it to me instead, I'll take the burden of it.' And later Anny takes the X-ray right across no-man's-land and into the forest, where she buries it.

Let the wolves have it, these much-storied wolves.

Now, Anny wonders what happened after Papa spent the family's fortune. The hyperinflation would probably have eaten it away, in any case. This social sickness that destroyed money, disconnecting it from its metaphorical value and reducing it into constituent bits of metal and paper (just as a tubercular lesion eats away at the connecting structure of a previously healthy lung, rendering it into blood and isolated specks of tissue), hyperinflation had started while Anny and Erwin were in Arosa. Now, thinking of the circular marks of disease on the X-ray reminds Anny of equally small and completely worthless coins from the pre-hyperinflation era that she is still finding in the nooks and crannies of their Zurich apartment.

In her hotel room, Anny gets into the bath and surrenders to the comforting water. Ilse/Elsi might have recovered. People did. Erwin spent days, no – entire *weeks* bed-bound, feverish and breathless, reliant on jars of oxygen, propped up on pillows so he could be fed spoonfuls of broth. So. She might be fine. Anny dabbles her fingertips in the now-lukewarm bath water and shuts her eyes. She thinks of Ilse/Elsi with pink cheeks, laughing, effortlessly running up the mountain path, her arms full of flowers. What type? For no real reason Anny gives Ilse/Elsi deliciously scented hyacinths, and then leans back into the enamel embrace of the bathtub and shuts her eyes.

It is exhausting and requires constant effort, keeping someone alive in your mind.

In Arosa, Anny decides not to say anything more about the wolves to Ilse/Elsi when a memory arises unbidden from seven, eight, no, nine years ago: she's sitting on a beach, watching Erwin play cricket with his tutor's sons while his tutor's wife is murmuring, 'You are too young for him, Anny.'

Anny glances at Erwin as he pounces for the ball, knocking over the wicket and scattering the bales everywhere to the delighted screams of the boys. 'He's twenty-two,' she says, 'only six years older than me.'

The other woman hesitates, 'He likes you *because* you are too young, do you understand what I'm saying?'

It's later that same day when the two of them touch for the first time. He runs his hands down the thick plait of her hair, slipping his fingers into the ins and outs of it until he reaches the bottom and she watches (as if it belongs to someone else) the velvet bow being caressed between his fingertips until, finally, as she catches her breath, the knot is undone, and under the pressure of his fingers, it works its way loose into a long red streak, and her hair falls apart. Then he rolls up the ribbon and tucks it into his jacket pocket, and winks a secret complicit silence at her.

When the holiday is over, they write to each other. She from her family home near Graz, he from where his regiment is stationed on the Karst. She used to think that these letters were banknotes, a promise of future pleasure.

And just look at what the hyperinflation did to banknotes.

In Zurich, Anny knows that Erwin will get it wrong. Not straightaway, not obviously. At first he will think that he, and he alone, has been revealed the truth of the atom. It is only later, after the triumphant return to his university department, after the promotion and the burgeoning friendships with Einstein and Planck, that doubts will surface like coughs from an apparently healthy person.

But for now, she casts Erwin into a mixture of heightened emotions. The work is progressing, each day is marked by a mathematical development that unfolds like the deciphering of a code, and he is beginning to see the atom as it should be seen. No longer a miniature solar system with a nucleus surrounded by orbiting electron-particles at arbitrary distances, it is now a system of connected waves whose properties can, thanks to him, all be predicted from first principles, using a single straightforward equation. And when he finishes work each evening, he tries to relax and enjoy himself. This is not so easy when he is still persistently coughing.

He cannot stop himself from repeatedly inspecting his face in the mirror, searching for the telltale symptoms; a hectic and fevered flush to the cheeks, a brilliance to the eyes, a general heightening of the senses. He has just the right sort of temperament for the illness, although he is aware of how unscientific this sounds.

Until the physiological cause of tuberculosis was identified as bacilli (and, interestingly, for some time afterwards), certain types of people were judged to be inherently more susceptible to it than others; sensitive types, dreamers, people attuned to their surroundings. The last time Erwin was diagnosed, his experience was marked by sensations of sinking, of drowning in air. Ordinary life seemed to be giving way to something more special and more heightened. For Hans Castorp, his illness is a direct conduit to developing a sexual obsession with fellow patient Clawdia Chauchat. For Erwin, suffering from tuberculosis has always felt a little like falling in love, in which there is no beloved other than the disease itself. He has learnt to lie in bed with his disease and allow it to caress him while he succumbs to its touch. What is more erotic than the lick of death?

Schrödinger commented on his equation that it was 'very beautiful'. In fact it's an asynchronous oddity, an inharmonious chord, a melding together of bits of classical and quantum physics in a way that cannot be rigorously derived, only postulated. This mathematical description of electron energies takes the form of a 'wave equation', a decidedly nineteenth-century concept in which quantum physics makes only a brief appearance in the shape of that single letter h: Planck's constant. Schrödinger's understanding of the world was a common-sense one in which reality is persistently 'out there', and we are able to record it (through our experiments) and describe it (with our theories) as if we are no more than scientific ghosts, making no impression on what we see.

On a practical level the equation worked perfectly; furthermore, it looked similar enough to earlier wave equations for people to be able to forget or dismiss, at least initially, its odd quantum-classical hybridity and the associated problems with deciphering it. Did it mean what it appeared to be saying on the surface, namely, that electrons were actually waves (and not particles)? Or was this just a metaphor, a consequence of the maths that had been used to express it?

In any case, it soon started to unravel. Electrons orbiting atoms might well be standing waves, but electrons freed from those constraints, such as those liberated by X-rays, were definitely particles, and on photographic plates they appeared as pinpoints.

Before it actually happened, Anny thought that marriage would be laughter and flirtation and fun. But soon after their wedding, death entered their marital home and never left. Perhaps it even started before that, with the discussions about the honeymoon.

'Not Duino,' Erwin said when she suggested this place to him. It was a popular holiday resort, just up the coast from Trieste. 'Anywhere but Duino.' And when she asked him what was wrong with it, he told her about Boltzmann.

'My physics lecturer died there,' and Erwin explained how this sudden death in 1906 cast a pall over his first days as a physics student at the University of Vienna, the classes having to be rearranged, substitute lecturers brought in at the last minute. The students sitting hushed and quiet through the derivation of the second law of thermodynamics and explanations of entropy. Even the idea of atoms, Boltzmann's great and controversial idea of matter being constituted of atoms too small to detect but which never-theless obeyed statistical laws, was now tainted with death.

Anny couldn't see what this had to do with where they went on honeymoon. It would have been better if Erwin had explained from the off that Boltzmann had not just died at Duino, but committed suicide. While his wife and daughter were enjoying themselves by the shore, he slipped away and found a tree and hanged himself.

And so it was in the midst of this argument that Erwin introduced to Anny the concept of entropy. Glaring at her as he scribbled down the second law of thermodynamics (the mathematical equivalent to stating that entropy/disorder must stay constant or increase with the passing of time), he explained the universal slide towards a monot-onous dark state as disorder piles up around us. And yet it was not an utter certainty. In some corner of the universe Boltzmann proved there was a small chance that tea-cups smashed in anger reassembled themselves, and that spouses would remain faithful to each other all their lives.

But that place was very far away from Anny and Erwin.

The purchase of the wedding ring was another instance that should have been a joyful moment and yet foreboded death. They were standing in a small jeweller's shop not far from St Stephen's right in the centre of Vienna, and the kindly and rather elderly Jewish man behind the counter was smiling as Anny gazed down at the rows of rings. She couldn't really see much difference between them, a gold band is a gold band but it was the idea that mattered. However, Erwin was not taking as much interest as he might have done, so it was up to Anny to conduct a lengthy chat with the jeweller about carats.

'Look, Erwin!' A delicate ring shone as steadily as her love for him, as she stretched out her hand but he didn't look, he just gazed out of the window at a group of fashionably dressed and fashionably thin women. And she felt very young and foolish, standing there in her old school coat. When he did finally turn to her, he gripped her hand so hard that the metal bit into her skin, and she almost cried out. The next day her fingers were bruised.

And so it was that Anny learnt the next lesson, about Röntgen who made the world's first X-ray image in 1895 when his wife allowed her hand to be placed on a photographic plate and bombarded with X-rays. And what did Frau Röntgen say when she saw the bones, the metacarpals, the knuckles? *I have seen my own death.* Nobody knows what else she said, how she may or may not have expounded on the subject of viewing her own body through the medium of invisible rays produced by her husband. And whether she blamed her husband for this unlooked-for knowledge, even after he was awarded the first Nobel Prize in physics for this discovery. Anny thinks of Frau Röntgen as an unwitting collaborator in an ongoing experiment she has no control over, which is perhaps the most accurate description of marriage that she's yet found.

In Zurich, the hotel goes about its daily ritual; breakfast is served, eaten and cleared away. Rooms are swept, money makes its way from the guests' hands to the proprietress's. And Anny realises Ilse/Elsi never offered any actual proof of her twin's existence. Anny simply believed what she was told. She cannot even envisage Ilse/Elsi beyond the boundaries of Arosa, just as in *The Magic Mountain* the reader loses sight of Hans Castorp after his sojourn at the sanatorium ends in 1914. (All we're told is that he joins the army and goes off to fight on the Western Front. After that he is probably – given the grim statistics – lost in the mud.)

In Arosa, the X-rays continue to be developed in the basement darkroom. Small squares of glass capture the secret insides of patients. The to-ings and fro-ings of viscera, organs, muscles and bones are all transformed onto a static surface that can be used to predict the future more surely than a pack of cards.

Perhaps part of Frau Röntgen's shock derives from witnessing a semi-fictional event (who, after all, is able to believe in their own death?) that has been plucked out of the future and merged into the present moment. And this merging equally fuses together the act of experiencing death and commenting on it. Frau Röntgen is rendered an observer of her own experience, both object and subject of an experiment. There is a circularity to viewing yourself in an X-ray and asking *is this me?*, a circularity that nevertheless splits you into two.

Anny knows that Erwin will be dutifully writing to her each day, as he always does when he is away from home, at an academic conference, say. Perhaps a card depicting the Arosa hotel in mid-winter, picturesque in its snowy overcoat, and on the back a line or two dashed off before the maid comes to collect the post: 'Weather marvellously invigorating!' or 'Having a productive time' or 'Met some old acquaintances'.

Normally she would reply to him, filling page after page with domestic trivia about muddled-up butcher's orders and infestations of pantry moths and the charwoman's troubles with her stepsons. All of it a front, a charade. Anny has learnt to play her part, and can do it so well even in the disappointed theatre of their home.

Now, she doesn't write back. The cards from Arosa will be piling up in their postbox, unseen, unread. Erwin's irritation at her failure to respond will, after a few days, shade into annoyance and then, after a few more days, into worry. Let him worry. Let him, for once, be aware that she may not be totally predictable. That the creature he married does not exist just to respond to him. She'd send him a blank postcard, if this might not also be interpreted as a white flag of surrender. Yes, not writing to him is the best way of making him wonder, even if just momentarily. Long enough for a flicker of doubt about her to be registered in his brain.

Anny fashions a likely future for her husband out of the materials she has available: playing cards and closed pianos and the hidden rooms of basements. As a result of his equation, Schrödinger will succeed Planck and become professor of physics in Berlin. But the arguments about the actual meaning of his equation will not stop, and indeed Max Born at Göttingen University soon proposes a quite different interpretation. According to Born, the wave in the equation is not an actual physical one, but rather a mathematical wave that can be used to calculate the possibility of the electron being in certain locations at certain times. In Born's view, before you observe it, the electron might be

here, or

here, or

here.

It is only when the observation is made that this probability wave 'collapses' and a specific value can be recorded.

Max Born's interpretation rapidly becomes accepted amongst physicists. But it simply shifts the nature of the problem, now we no longer have to worry about what the electron actually is, but we do have to worry about what constitutes an observation. Does this happen when the equipment mechanically records the electron, or is a human being required?

Anny knows a human being is always involved, even if they are not physically present. Max Born's ideas of probability waves are borrowed from the unknown and unseen fate of the girl and her twin as a result of their papa's gambling. Schrödinger's riposte, that this is as absurd as a cat imprisoned in a box being simultaneously both dead and alive, does not seem at all absurd to Anny, who has to endure the ongoing presence of the piano-that-is-not-a-piano.

Max Planck reads about Schrödinger's equation and Born's interpretation and is reminded of his long-dead daughters. He is all too aware that he did not give enough attention to Emma and Grete when they were young. During much of their childhood(s), they had to keep each other company; their brothers were sent away to school while they remained at home in the big house surrounded by the ancient Grunewald forest to the west of Berlin. Here they played at being the heroines in Grimms' tales: spinning straw into gold, getting the better of wolves until they were deemed too old to be heroines and had to become young ladies.

Emma was the first to get married. She gave birth to her daughter, and promptly died. Her grieving husband took Grete as his wife and to help him bring up Emma's daughter/Grete's niece. But it must have been like marrying the ghost of his first wife; Grete smelt of earth, she tasted of stone, the only thing that was hers and not Emma's were the gaps between her thin fingers, the wind whistling through them like it did through the tall trees in the graveyard where Emma was buried. And Grete spent the rest of her short and numbered days sitting beneath a portrait of Emma garlanded in black ribbons – until she too had a daughter and she too died in giving birth.

Daughters keep transforming themselves into more daughters and so on all the way down the periodic table, which is simply another way of writing hope.

It is time to leave the hotel/sanatorium. Erwin boards an already crowded train and heads back to Zurich, sitting amongst the holidaymakers and their skis, his mind still on the equation. Anny goes to the lobby and pays the bill before she boards the tram back to the apartment, or –

It is time to extend the argument because it is not enough to say 'Every book written about Schrödinger notes his charm, his ease with people. Many books comment on his attraction to women, and his appreciation of them.' Now, it's necessary to add: a few books note his being drawn to young women. One or two books tell us that he had to be warned off approaching young girls. When reading the official biography, it's hard not to feel a queasy admixture of being impressed by his science and repulsed by his overtures to twelve-year-olds. All through his life, whenever he wanted to pacify Anny, he would make a gesture as if stroking her plait of hair, long disappeared. The biography refers to his 'Lolita Complex', a tortured phrase that avoids addressing what is in plain sight.

When Anny arrives back at their apartment, she discovers Erwin standing quite still, facing his grandfather in the parlour. The postcards he sent to her are still piled in the postbox, the air in the apartment is both cold and stale. There's no fresh bread or milk. And he's not feeling well, he has a cough, it might mean something. He had to consult the doctor in the hotel.

His voice is querulous. She brews him some coffee, then she goes to the bedroom and lays a clean eiderdown on the bed for him. He follows her.

'I discovered something in Arosa. Something about the atom.'

'Any atom in particular?' She means this as a serious question and is slightly affronted when he laughs.

Nothing's changed. Carry on. Erwin has a disturbing coughing fit each morning and yet he can still run up a flight of stairs with the speed of a goat. The illness is both there and not there. Their marriage is both real and imaginary. Now and then she wipes the dust from the surface of the piano.

Let's open that piano. Perhaps when Anny leaves the hotel in Zurich, she doesn't get onto the tram that carries her back to the apartment, but makes her way to the station, where she buys a ticket for a train travelling north, quite the opposite direction to Arosa.

Later, as she's watching Switzerland slide away from her, she pictures Erwin in the apartment by himself. She makes him sit at the opened piano, and strike the keys in a discordant and inharmonious manner. She makes him wince at the noise he has made, and yet he is compelled to repeat it, each out-of-tune chord growing louder and louder, until the ornaments rattle in protest. Schrödinger is immobile at the piano, unable to move away, only his fingers have any sort of life to them.

Now Anny imagines herself in the cold parlour by Erwin's side as he tells her they will move to Berlin. His work has been welcomed by other physicists and he has been offered a professorship. Finally he has made it. Anny sees Erwin pat her hand in a friendly manner, as one might pat a pet dog, before asking her to brew him yet another cup of coffee. Anny sees that other Anny inside the apartment, her head turned away from her husband as he talks endlessly about this and that.

Yes, there is a problem with terminology, decides Anny. We persist in calling an entity x, when in fact it might be something quite different, but we're just not equipped to understand it, not yet. What is labelled a 'friendship' between an older man and a young girl is nothing of the sort, might be better termed 'unhealthy obsession' or 'abuse'.

By the time her train reaches Hamburg, she can predict Erwin approaching a whole series of girls. She can predict an unpleasant scene on a beach, where a man will threaten to call the police after his twelve-year-old daughter complains that Erwin has been trying to talk to her. And an awkward discussion in which a Catholic priest will take Erwin aside and warn him off pursuing the daughter of a family friend. And a teenager who is impregnated by him and gives birth to a daughter.

And Anny won't ever know for sure, but we are allowed to know that Ilse/Elsi survived her illness and left the sanatorium in Arosa. She will slip from view by becoming a photographer, by staking her position behind the camera, wherever that may be. Ilse/Elsi is a most unobtrusive photographer who captures her subjects without them realising. To be sure, these people are rendered unrecognisable and not much more than interferences of light.

Part of my job requires me to make a virtual tour of the entire complex of laboratories, offices and workshops, allowing me to pass through locked doors and into chambers which are normally forbidden the real version of me. This way I can get up close to signs hung on walls depicting cartoon atoms, I can zip right through the protective lead shield and hover around the radioactive source. One moment I'm standing outside in the carpark, where the building's matrix of shiny windows reflects uniform sunlight at me, the next moment I'm far underground, immersed in a tangle of wires and cables, before I whizz at an impossibly high velocity around the famous circular tunnel. Other people appear and disappear but they're ethereally frozen in time and space; in my universe I'm the only one who's able to move.

Once a week I carry out this tour to make sure everything's still working, that all the captions and cutaway diagrams of the experiments are up to date, so that other people can follow in my footsteps and see for themselves what we do here. In an organisation that's responsible for the most complex experiments ever attempted, using billions of tax payers' money to do them, transparency is all-important. And it doesn't matter that I've never walked the tunnel in real life, I bet Peter Higgs hasn't either.

The rest of the time I'm working out how to explain atoms and nuclear decay and leptons and bosons and carrier forces, and all the rest of the jargon:

When a radioactive atom of element X decays into a daughter atom of element Y, nothing connects Y to its parent atom X. Daughter atoms show no trace of their origins. They may in turn be radioactive and decay further.

Why *daughters* and *parents*? Who thought of that metaphor? I've grown to dislike it in this context, the way it's linked to decay, to mutation. My mum was always so energetic and lively. Even when she was ill, people commented on how healthy she still looked. As if that was helping her.

It is impossible to predict in advance when exactly an individual atom will decay. All that is known is the 'half-life', the time in which half the atoms in a collective ensemble will mutate into their daughters.

I'd prefer the word 'transform' to 'decay' or 'mutate', it seems more hopeful, but it isn't standard scientific language. At the last meeting with Mum's consultant, he'd given her three months but she'd lasted five. That was something to be grateful for.

Whenever I meet someone new, I tell them that I get paid to make up stories about particles. Stories that are balanced between the past and the future, between what we already know and what we want to know, because every new revelation must be contrasted by a promise of more to come, this is the eternal law of science communication. As well as making clear that the scientists are never at the end of their work, and that everything we believe now might be ridiculed in the future.

Today my work is interrupted by a freelance photographer making a visit to take photos of the latest experiment. When the phone rings to ask if I can come to reception, I'm in no hurry; I've met too many photographers in the past, so I give it ten minutes before setting off. Let him wait.

He arrives well before the agreed time because he was anxious about the journey. The interface between CERN and the surrounding world is difficult to navigate; signs on the motorway are confusing, arrows pointing one way and then the other. He can spot the cluster of buildings outlined against the sky but they never seem to get any nearer until, all at once, he's driving around the visitors' carpark.

At reception he shows his ID, and the man behind the reception desk holds up one finger, and disappears to consult with someone else invisible behind a door.

He waits. People come and go, looking as if they know their place here. He imagines them sinking down beneath the surface of this building, tunnelling through the soil past the worms and rocks and tree roots, where they find glowing particles as beautiful as diamonds. He's aware this is fanciful nonsense.

Hanging from the ceiling of the reception are vast pictures of scientific equipment: metal tubes, wires, cages, computer screens, a spider's web of cables emanating from a tunnel into a cavernous underground hall. After a bit, all the different words for 'big' seem superfluous because everything is big here, apart from the actual subjects of the experiments. They're the tiniest things conceivable.

He checks the time again, he's now late and the receptionist still hasn't returned. He looks at the images of particles, wondering what he's actually looking at. Photos of computer screens, images of images. It has the effect of furthering reality, making all the bosons and quarks and everything else seem even more distant from everyday life, rather than bringing them within the human realm. Whatever bosons and quarks are, they're definitely not colourful lines on an electronic display.

A woman is standing in front of him, as if his unconscious has summoned her. 'Ready to go?' she says. He nods. The receptionist finally reappears and says 'Have a nice day.' But he's not sure about the concept of days in a place that must be carefully shielded from all sunshine. Here, a day is nothing more than a certain number of atomic oscillations, and he wonders what this does to other aspects of normal life, and whether they get transformed into similarly abstract entities.

The latest result is the discovery of a new particle. It was predicted many years ago, and now that CERN has determined some of its essential attributes, the particle has crossed the barrier from theoretical to actual. To be sure, the particle's lifetime is fabulously short, just a matter of milliseconds. Nevertheless, that is measurable and so the particle can be said to exist. As I explain this to the photographer, I wonder just how much the particle is able to experience, perhaps it's the atomic equivalent of a mayfly, birth, love and death occurring all at once. But it's the centre of its universe.

'You know how they determined the lifetime of this particle?' I don't wait for him to reply before I continue, 'They measured the length of its track on the detector.' I point at one of the many infographics on the wall, an image of fireworks, of lines both straight and curved spiralling out of a central point. The image is an aftershock of an explosion that brings particles to life before destroying them. 'You can only calculate its lifetime after it's died.' I'm still in caption-writing mode.

Now that Mum has gone, I'm the one who has to deal with her belongings. She worked as a fashion designer and in all of the many items abandoned in the studio – the sheaves of paper patterns, the folded lengths of fabric and the rattling drawers of cotton reels – I can trace her life's work. When I picked up the dressmaker's scissors and realised they fit my fingers perfectly, I allowed myself to pretend I'd inherited her ability. But the scissors opened and shut on empty air, and the patterns flapped in the breeze, and I knew I would never be able to use them, their essential purpose now as outdated as a treadle-operated sewing machine.

All of these belongings relate to her work – apart from one. Underneath her bed, which had been her sickbed and then, during a short but unknowable period of time one Sunday evening in the middle of March, transformed into her deathbed, I found a large brown envelope. The sort that might contain a certificate for an academic qualification. Congratulations, it might say, in curly writing. Except this brown envelope contains an X-ray.

He doesn't like scientists' talk of *lifetimes*, their professional glee in determining the essential aspects of a particle after it's gone. Prefers the indeterminacy of *half-lives*, of not knowing when an individual particle will blink out of existence, give up one mask of reality for another. Change from mass to energy, or back again. This is what he's been led to believe it's all about, some sort of exchange in a manner we can only glimpse.

'Be careful and follow me, because it's easy to get lost,' she tells him now, 'even though the place is essentially a vast circle, the main beam is diverted out of the main tunnel to all the different experiments, and each of them has their own set of labs. You have to take care,' she repeats because he's looking through his camera at a section of shiny sinuous piping that appears to have burst through the wall. When he swivels back in her direction he's still looking through his camera, and he notices how she recoils from his cyclops gaze.

They enter a lift, a large clanking box similar to those in hospitals that are used to convey bodies both alive and dead. As they descend further than he would have thought possible, she says something to him, but her words are partly muffled by the mechanical noise and what he hears is 'Welcome to hell'. The lift shudders and pauses, and he thinks how ironic it would be if they got stuck in a broken-down lift in one of the world's most high-tech labs. But then it accelerates downwards and he feels a weightless sensation in his stomach.

When they finally emerge, she indicates a map on the wall. *You are here* is marked with a red sticker on a labyrinth he has no hope of deciphering. He hadn't realised the place was so large, that there were so many locked doors to forbidden chambers where equipment that's both delicate and dangerous is carrying out its relentless tasks. As they walk along the corridor, people pass them by and nod at the woman, and don't pay any attention to him.

However, and in spite of the unease he felt in the lift, he's exhilarated. There's a sense that nothing is incidental. Everything has a purpose, a role to play in the unravelling of the spools of matter inside them all. Even a wooden crate apparently abandoned in the corridor could, if you traced its history, reveal something of the nature of the universe. He feels somehow revived after the difficult journey and the taciturn nature of his guide, and he darts off to look at informatics, at screens he can't hope to understand, at equipment he can't name and whose function he can't guess. Once he almost trips over a gaggle of students crowded around a circuit board.

They walk along corridor after corridor, past door after door, and the woman always remains a few steps in front of him so that all he can see of her is the back of her head. She doesn't turn to check he's following, nor does she say anything. It's her function to lead him where he needs to be, that is all, this is what her manner of walking conveys to him. As he walks in her footsteps, he realises that he's indeed reliant on her. All the corridors look alike, and apart from the baffling maps, there are no clues to orientate them. Nothing has penetrated from above ground to indicate where they are, whether they are still directly below the cluster of buildings that make up the main part of CERN or if they have already travelled out beyond its limits, and are standing underneath a field or a small French village.

After walking for what feels like hours, they arrive at the door to the LHC. This is it, the centre of it all.

'Omphalos,' he murmurs, and he's surprised when she glances at him as if she understands.

She has barely spoken since the lift but now she replies, 'The navel of the universe,' and she nods at him as if they're equals in some obscure arithmetic.

When I found the X-ray under her bed, I held it up to the bedroom window as if making an offering to the sunlight, and saw the spinal column as precise and tessellated as some architectural model, each vertebrae clicked into place. The organs themselves were altogether less distinctive, shadowy suggestions of a liver or a uterus. Numerous dark patches were carelessly sprinkled around, with some of the larger ones indicated by arrows drawn in felt-tip so that anyone – not just a medical expert – could understand that they were looking at budding tumours.

I don't know why Mum even had this X-ray, why she'd brought it home from the hospital. But perhaps she needed some sort of external evidence of what was going on inside her. Perhaps it indicated a hope that her medical treatment was not yet exhausted, that there were still options, that she still had a future. I replaced it where I'd found it, because I couldn't think what else to do with it.

Now I've come to think of it as the monster beneath the bed. Unseen, yet ever-present.

'No,' she says, 'I'm sorry, I can't.' Straightaway she regrets saying 'sorry'. The thing is impossible, though.

'Why?' he's perplexed, 'I just need someone in the frame because otherwise viewers won't be able to tell how large or small the equipment is. They need to see something they can relate to.'

'I can't,' she repeats, 'after all, you don't need an actual person. A bicycle or… a skeleton would do just as well.'

'A skeleton?' What on earth is she talking about?

'I thought you weren't actually going to do any photography today. Didn't you describe this visit as simply a reconnaissance, to work out possible future tactics?'

He nods. 'And for that I have to take preliminary shots, to help work out the final ones.' He always needs photos, that is how he orientates his way through the world. His childhood memories are of physical pictures, or have constituted themselves as pictures, he can't tell the difference anymore. It's easy to substitute longed-for memories with Kodak prints. In one, a young man stands grinning with a small boy balanced on his bare shoulders. But the photo's too blurred and too small to be able to identify them accurately, you'd have to know who they are.

They've paused in front of a notice board with an array of photos showing the staff and technicians responsible for this particular lab. Each face is the same size and angled the same direction, each person is smiling the same calm and competent smile. It doesn't matter that they're women, men, old, young and of various ethnicities; there's a uniform reality to them that is artificial, constructed by the camera. He should know, he's constructed artificial realities himself, many times.

I can't explain why it's impossible, why I can't have my photograph taken by him. And actually I've already hinted at it, with my explanation of how the particle's lifetime is determined. If he remembers me saying this, he should understand. I'm not telling him anything about the X-ray. I'm not.

Mum never really understood what I did for a living. She didn't study science at school so she knew nothing about cells or genes or DNA, but she died of the same disease that killed Rosalind Franklin. A cancer that starts in the ovaries, that mimics pregnancy. Apparently people kept asking Rosalind Franklin if she was expecting. Mum said it felt like carrying a stone baby. A disease that gives birth to death.

Although she's obviously upset, the light on her face is rather interesting. The light source itself is awful, the flat and dull glare of overhead fluorescent tubes. But her skin is doing something to it, transforming it in a way he didn't think possible, bringing out different colours and tones and giving her face the appearance of a Hollywood movie star from the forties, he can't think who exactly. A face made enormous on the poster outside a cinema, a face that is metamorphosed into sunlit planes and shadowed valleys. But he knows he can't explain this to her without upsetting her further. Honestly, what is her problem?

'I could delete the photos later, once I've used them to calculate what I need. Exposure times and f-stops. Would that help?'

She looks at him, even more aghast.

I haven't cried since Mum's funeral. It's all sealed up inside me, hidden away. When I'm not working here, I have to go to her house and deal with the seemingly endless belongings, the clothes and shoes and jewellery and fabric and wool and little bits of kit I can't use. Hole punchers? Pinking shears? Overlockers? The names of these items float back to me from my childhood. Mum had more stuff than I thought possible, each wardrobe and suitcase reveals its hidden contents, gives up its secrets like the atoms riding the tunnels at CERN.

And I'm as rigorous and thorough as any scientist. I check the pockets of a mackintosh not worn since the 1960s and find an apparent shopping list; *Tins toms, marge? Post office!* That's decipherable, but *Jess? No!* and ~~Mark~~ *haha* are a code I can't hope to crack. I find long-abandoned handbags made from skins of animals that are no longer legally culled. I sort through cracked lipsticks in colours that have surely altered with age, just as Mum's hair evolved from blonde to auburn until finally it was transformed into a grey fuzz on a scalp revealed by chemotherapy.

Initially I thought I would keep what I liked and simply give the rest away, but too much is piled in limbo on the workroom floor, waiting for me to decide its fate, and I find that I can't.

An atom may or may not mutate. An atom with a predicted half-life of eight minutes, may, an hour later, still have retained its old identity, in spite of everything around it being utterly different.

'Look,' he's trying to sound reasonable. 'More photos are better than fewer photos, surely?'

She seems puzzled by this.

'More photos means more information, and that's always a good thing.' But she still seems wary, as if she doesn't want to turn her back on him again in case he surreptitiously takes her photo. And he realises that she will keep her gaze trained on him until he leaves the building, she won't look away, because somehow he has betrayed her with his insistence on capturing her image. Trapping her in his camera.

If he takes a photo of me, some of the light emitted by the fluorescent tubes high above the two of us would hit my face and be reflected towards his camera lens, which would focus this light onto a digital array of pixels, the vertical layers of which are sensitive to blue, green and red light respectively. This array would convert the light at these different wavelengths into an electrical charge which would then, pixel by pixel, be read out and stored as a sequence of ones and zeros in the camera's memory.

If a member of the public asked me how a digital camera works, that's how I'd explain it.

This is also what I know: that someone who sees this photo will be able to analyse it as thoroughly as that of a sub-atomic particle, to quantify the hue of my skin, the colour of my irises, and consequently calculate my future death.

I have a half-life in this underground place that gives me shelter. And a half-life is better than none at all.

'Alright,' he says, surprising himself, 'don't worry. I'll do it another way.' And already his mind is thinking through possible different ways of showing the relationship between the lab equipment and their human operators. Perhaps he could be more subtle about it, use a note book and pencil to indicate scale. He turns away from her, and spots a lab coat hanging from its hook. What comes to mind is the image of the young man balancing the small boy on his shoulders. Was the man actually grinning? Could you see his teeth in the photo?

'Thank you.'

'Alright,' he repeats. 'I know what it's like,' which surprises him again, because really he has no idea what he's referring to.

'It's just, you don't know what's in a photo, do you? What information is encrypted in the light levels, the shapes...'

He nods. The particle tracks don't peter out, they don't predict what will happen, they just stop, and these sudden endings are disturbing. The image of the young man with the boy doesn't give any indication about the disappearance of that man after he left the boy at a roadside café on the way home from a day out. It wasn't far from here, he remembers, at least not in terms of geographical distance. A swim, an ice cream, an argument about a forgotten towel. That's what he remembers, and then nothing more until he was found by his mother, sitting at a table by himself in the café, drinking a fizzy pop and waiting.

He's still waiting. Why that café, he wonders. Was it just the sudden culmination of a secret desire to escape? Or was it something he said or did that triggered it? The forgotten towel?

He doesn't have the photo anymore, his mum threw it out along with the rest of his dad's belongings, and he wouldn't recognise his dad now if they passed each other in the street. But it doesn't stop him taking photos everywhere he goes. Even down here below ground.

We ride the lift to the surface, standing side by side in silence because I'm too preoccupied by memories to say anything. When she was X-rayed, Mum was transformed into a particle accelerator; radiation travelled through her, scattering off her bones and organs. Even when she was still alive, the X-ray became a ghost that haunted our house. The only thing to do now is to remove it from that temporary Hades under the bed, and give it a proper burial. I'll dig a hole, lay the final image of her in the earth and scatter soil over her.

When they get the lift back up to the reception, he realises she's no longer looking at him but staring straight ahead. He wants to know more about the photo in her mind, but doesn't want to speak and break the silence that grows like trust.

At the entrance to the lab, I surprise myself by shaking his hand, and I turn away before he leaves and goes out into the world where sunshine is permissible.

Notes on Stories

Alternative geometries: Valentina Tereshkova really did visit the Royal Observatory Edinburgh in 1990, and I really did meet her.

Yellow: As part of her PhD in the 1950s, Margaret Bastock studied the relationship between behaviour, genetics and evolution using the fruit fly *Drosophila melanogaster*. She was the first scientist to publish evidence of a single gene influencing behaviour.

Footnotes to a scientific paper concerning the possible detection of a neutrino[1]: The strange story of the particle physicist Bruno Pontecorvo, and whether he was a Soviet spy or just a committed Communist, is told by Frank Close in *Half-Life: The Divided Life of Bruno Pontecorvo, Physicist or Spy* (Oneworld, 2015).

The first and last expeditions to Antarctica: The documentary *Wende im Eis* (dir. Anna Schmidt) tells the real-life story of the 1989 East German mission to Antarctica, with contributions from some of the women who participated in the pioneering West German mission.

Mrs McLean and Margaret are now in charge: 'Margaret' is Margaret Burbidge (1919–2020), the astrophysicist who, together with Geoffrey Burbidge (her husband), Frank Hoyle and Willy Fowler, did the groundbreaking work that explained how heavy chemical elements are generated by nuclear fusion in the centres of stars. During the Second World War, she looked after the University of London's Mill Hill Observatory, and later she became the first woman director of the Royal Greenwich Observatory. There is no trace of Mrs McLean in the records of the Mill Hill Observatory.

DISTANT RELATIVES OF THE SAMSA FAMILY: The real-life Institute for Typhus and Virus Research was initiated by Rudolph Weigl in Lemberg/Lwów/Lviv in 1920, and subsequently helped to protect its Jewish volunteers during the Nazi occupation of Ukraine.

SAFETY MANOEUVRES: The interactions between NASA technicians and the Mars rovers operated by them are described in *Seeing Like a Rover* by Janet Vertesi (University of Chicago Press, 2015).

SCHRÖDINGER'S WIFE: *Schrödinger: Life and Thought* by Walter Moore (Cambridge University Press, 1989) is the standard biography, which describes Schrödinger abandoning Anny in December 1925 to go away on holiday by himself to Arosa, where he meets a mystery lover, an incident that too many subsequent commentators refer to unquestioningly. But if you follow the paper trail of references in Moore's book, you discover that there's no real evidence, only hearsay.

Acknowledgements

I gratefully acknowledge the editors of literary journals and other outlets in which versions of these stories first appeared:

'ALTERNATIVE GEOMETRIES' in *Litro*.

'YELLOW' was first published as 'Considering the role of the female' in *Tamarind*.

'A UNIVERSAL EXPLANATION OF TOAST' in *The Phare*.

'THE EXPERT IN PAIN' in *The Fiction Pool*.

'FOOTNOTES TO A SCIENTIFIC PAPER CONCERNING THE POSSIBLE DETECTION OF A NEUTRINO[1]' in *Riggwelter*.

'UNSETTLED' in the anthology *Home is Elsewhere* by The Reader Berlin.

'AN INVESTIGATION INTO LOVE BY BABCOCK AND WAINWRIGHT' was broadcast on BBC Radio 4 and published in *Lablit*.

'THE SHORTEST ROUTE ON THE MAP IS NOT THE QUICKEST' in the anthology *I Am Because You Are* by Freight Books.

'WELCOME TO PLANET ALBA™!' in the anthology *Scotland in Space* by Shoreline of Infinity.

Some of these stories were written when I was a writer-in-residence in the 'fiction meets science' programme hosted at the Hanse-Wissenschaftskolleg in Delmenhorst, Germany, in 2014–15. Others were written during my ongoing residency at STIS (Science, Technology and Innovation Studies unit) at the University of Edinburgh. I'm very appreciative of the support of these institutions.

I'm very grateful to my writing and reading pals for providing advice, feedback and coffee, and being all-round good eggs, particularly Mary Paulson-Ellis, Tania Hershman, Eris Young, Noel Chidwick, Fadhila Mazanderani, Susan M. Gaines and Zoë Beck. I'm also grateful to Sarah Kember, Susan Kelly, Angela Thompson and the whole team at Goldsmiths Press/Gold SF. A big thank-you to my family, who have been endlessly kind and supportive: Herb Goldschmidt and Elaine Axby, Belle Brett and John Heymann and most of all Graeme.

The Gold SF series

Gold SF is a new imprint dedicated to discovering and publishing new intersectional feminist science fiction. Science fiction looks to the future and tries to imagine new ways of being in the world. Goldsmiths Press is a natural home for speculative fiction, and this new imprint promotes voices answering to our unprecedented times.

Empathy

9781913380618

Hoa Pham

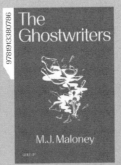

The Ghostwriters

9781913380786

M.J. Maloney

The Other Shore

9781913380823

Hoa Pham

Mathematics for Ladies

Poems on Women in Science

9781913380489

Jessy Randall

Merchant

9781915983053

Alexandra Grunberg

Little Sisters and Other Stories

9781915983077

Vonda N. McIntyre

The Disinformation War

9781913380809

S. J. Groenewegen

Schrödinger's Wife (and other possibilities)

9781915983183

Pippa Goldschmidt

The Headland

9781915983121

Abi Curtis

GOLD SF°

Series editors *Una McCormack* and *Paul March-Russell*